quack

quack

anna humphrey

Albert Whitman & Company
Chicago, Illinois

In memory of Tracie Klaehn
and Pecky the Duck

Library of Congress Cataloging-in-Publication data
is on file with the publisher.

Text copyright © 2020 by Anna Humphrey
First published in the United States of America
in 2020 by Albert Whitman & Company
ISBN 978-0-8075-6706-7 (hardcover)
ISBN 978-0-8075-6705-0 (ebook)

Printed in the United States of America
10 9 8 7 6 5 4 3 2 1 LB 24 23 22 21 20

Jacket art copyright © 2020 by Albert Whitman & Company
Jacket art by Stevie Lewis
Graphics used on pages 108 and 142 copyright © by vectorpocket/Freepik
Design by Aphelandra Messer

For more information about Albert Whitman & Company,
visit our website at www.albertwhitman.com.

quack

friends of the environment club

Meeting Date: May 29
Activity: Upcycle a Craft Creation!

When we can't reduce our waste or recycle it, the next best strategy is to reuse it! Today we'll talk about how reusing is a fun way to be friendly to planet Earth!

Let's find out what kinds of cool creations we can make out of old things like cardboard boxes, toilet paper rolls, tinfoil, drinking boxes, yogurt cups, and other common waste found around the school.

If we can dream them up, we can find ways to make them! Get to work, friends! Get creative... get crafty...and have fun!

CHAPTER 1

The Day of the Duck

Told by Pouya

People think my friend Shady is weird because he never talks at school. But so what? Weird is wonderful; that's what I say. Wacky's wonderful too—that's me.

Weird & wacky. Shady & me. We go together.

Plus, anyone who thinks Shady doesn't talk isn't paying attention. He talks all the time. Just not with words.

That day, we were on our way home from the Friends of the Environment after-school club when he slammed on his bike brakes and skidded sideways across the path.

Screeeeech!

See that? Shady talked loud and clear with his bike. He

yelled "STOOOOOP!" at the top of his lungs. I just didn't hear in time.

I ran straight into his back wheel, and both our bikes toppled sideways. Luckily, we're experienced fallers, so even though Shady scraped his elbow and my fingers got ker-slammed between our handlebars, neither of us made a big deal about it.

"Whoa. Dude. What's up?" I flexed my fingers to make sure the bendy parts still bent.

Shady pointed at a scruffy patch of grass to the side of the path. I was wearing a pair of X-ray–vision goggles that I'd upcycled out of old toilet paper rolls and some tinfoil at Environment Club. They looked pretty space-age, but they gave me tunnel vision. It was probably why I didn't see what he was talking about at first.

Shady had to point a second and then a third time. Finally, he dragged me over by the sleeve.

"Oh. I see them now." I crouched down.

There were three tiny ducklings wandering between the dandelions that had turned puffy and white. The ducklings were fluffy like the flowers and yellow and brown like the dead grass and dirt, so they blended in.

Shady's great at noticing stuff though. You should see him rip through a Where's Waldo? book. Because his mouth isn't busy talking, I think extra brainpower goes to his eyes.

He glanced left and right, pinching his lips together. Then he raised his eyebrows above the mirrored sunglasses he wears so kids at school won't look him in the eye.

"Uh-huh." I read his worried expression. "They're too little to be alone. Their duck mom's got to be around somewhere."

We peered under bushes and checked behind a garbage can. I even swung upside down from a low branch to get a different view and did a Tarzan impression. It made the corners of Shady's mouth turn up until he burst into a full smile.

Not surprisingly, he spotted her first. Shady tapped my shoulder and motioned with his head. There were so many cars whizzing past that I had to wait for a break in traffic to see for myself.

The mother duck—all the way on the other side of Dixon Road—had four more fluffy ducklings with her.

"She must have crossed to get to the water and left some behind," I said, spotting the drainage ditch on the far side.

Was it because I sensed, somehow, that this was a life-changing moment...or was it just what any true Friend of the Environment would do? Dunno. I just knew we needed to act.

"To the rescue!"

Shady gave me his A-OK sign: an almost invisible nod.

I crouched down on the grass, waddling and flapping my arms like wings as we chased ducklings. That made Shady laugh so hard his whole body vibrated like a boiling kettle, and I thought he might pee his pants. But those ducklings were in no mood to be caught. Every time we'd get our hands around one, it'd wriggle free and *boop* across the grass with its butt feathers wiggling double time.

At least three grown-ups walked past and looked at us like *we* were the animals, and an old lady carrying grocery bags yelled at us to "stop bothering the wildlife or I'll call the police." Luckily, she didn't have a cell phone with her, and the ice cream she'd just bought started melting, so she left.

"What do we do *now*?" I asked Shady. My head was getting sweaty, so I took off my bike helmet. That must have given Shady the idea.

He took off his helmet, too, letting his long hair fall over his face, then he waddled up to a dandelion and plopped the helmet down over it, to demonstrate.

"Killer move, Captain," I announced in a gravelly voice. It's from *The Evil Undead*—our favorite video game. The narrator says it every time we chop off the head of a zombie.

One of the ducklings was busy pecking something in the grass, and before it knew what was happening, I'd walked up beside it and plopped my helmet on top. "Gotcha, duck-a-roo!" I flipped the helmet upside down and scooped the duckling in.

The little guy stared up at me with beady, blinky black eyes. It quacked three times to let me know it was mad, but it didn't try to escape.

Shady caught one that way too.

But that still left one—and how were we supposed to trap it when we already had our hands full of ducklings in bike helmets?

Even though my X-ray vision goggles looked out of this world, it was time to admit that they weren't helping. I handed Shady my helmet and duckling and went to put the goggles in my backpack so I'd be able to see better. *That* was when I noticed the hunk of leftover lavash bread that one of my moms—probably Maman, but maybe Mitra-Joon—

had packed me for lunch. It was stuck to the bottom of my gym shoe.

Did ducks like extra-flattened Persian flatbread with a hint of gym-floor goo? It seemed worth a try.

I ripped off a little piece and threw it on the grass. "Here, ducky, ducky."

Like a zombie drawn to the scent of fresh guts, it couldn't resist. This was going to be easy.

"Watch this," I told Shady. I pulled out my math book and stood it upright to hold my backpack open. Then I laid a trail of lavash crumbs and hid behind a tree.

Boop, boop. Yum. Boop, boop. Yum.

The duckling ate its way right into my trap. I ran over, pulled out the math book, zipped my backpack closed, and pumped my fist in victory.

Now all we had to do was get three ducklings across four lanes of traffic.

Hoooooonk!

Squeal!

"Get off the road, idiots!"

"Where are your parents?"

You'd think we could have expected a "Thank you for

helping our city's wildlife!" but some drivers are all road rage and no manners. And things didn't get any better when we reached the other side.

Instead of being relieved to get her babies back, momma duck looked seriously upset. She was pacing back and forth, complaining loudly, like the lifeguards at the rec center do when we play human whack-a-mole with the pool noodles.

"It's okay, Miss Duck." I lowered my bike helmet to show her. "See? We've got your babies. Safe and sound."

She straightened her back, spread her wings, and beat them threateningly. Her black eyes had a cold, hard look.

Just then, Shady grabbed my arm and motioned back across the road.

"Not now, Shady," I said, but he tugged harder. "I said *not now...*" Then I saw them out of the corner of my eye. Two big kids—middle schoolers, at least—picking up our abandoned bikes.

"*Hey!*" I shouted—but if they heard me over the traffic, they didn't care. "Put those down!"

One of them swung his leg over the bar of Shady's bike and bonked the front wheel against the pavement, testing its bounce.

"Stop in the name of the law!" I yelled. I grabbed some pine cones off the grass and started hurling them across the street, but they all fell short. One bounced off the roof of a car that was speeding past.

That was when the mother duck—probably extra upset by all my yelling and chucking stuff—came right at us, flapping her wings in a frenzy.

Suddenly, our bikes getting stolen by teenagers didn't seem like the most important problem.

"Run for your life!" I yelled to Shady. But there was only one direction to go. Momma duck was between us and the road. Her beak was snapping like a pair of razor-sharp pincers.

Thunk, thunk, thunk, splash!

Me and Shady scrambled down the steep, grassy slope and into the murky, thigh-high, garbage-soup water of the drainage ditch.

The mother duck followed, flapping her wings and sending up a spray.

We dropped our helmets into the water. They filled through the holes and started to sink while the ducklings inside swam around like they were in little swimming pools. But even that didn't seem to satisfy Momma.

WAK! WAK! WAAAAAAK!

"Go! Go now! Before she pecks us to death."

I booted it, and I knew Shady was right behind me because I could hear the squashing, slapping sounds of his soaked sneakers beating double time as we scrambled up the other side of the ditch and dashed down the sidewalk to safety.

NEIGHBORHOOD WATCH NOTICE:
The Banana Bandit

There have been several police reports of the criminal known as "the Banana Bandit" striking in the areas of Summerside and Forest Hill. He is a Caucasian male in his mid-forties with dark hair and a goatee. He may or may not drive a black Mercedes Benz.

Most conspicuous, however, is the gorilla suit he wears. He tends to target middle-aged or elderly women, whom he surprises by throwing mashed bananas at before snatching their purses.

Please be cautious. If you see the Banana Bandit, do not approach. It can be difficult to predict how he might react. Be community-minded, but please do not take heroic measures. Rather, report the sighting to the local police or by calling the Neighborhood Watch tip line at 555-947-2214. Let's all work together to make our community a safe place to live, work, and play.

CHAPTER 2

The Dumbest Dumb Decision

Told by Manda

My brother, Shady, and his friend Pouya were late. *Really* late. And I'm in charge of keeping them alive between three thirty and five forty-five. So, of course, I was ready to kill them.

And fine. Obviously, I was worried too. When it comes to Shady, I'm always worried. *Everyone's* always worried. It's what we do.

Dad worries about him getting lost at the shopping mall or at the beach when we're on vacation—because how would he ask for help? Dad also worries about whether Shady will find a job one day if he doesn't start talking to people other than us. "There's a limited market for mimes," I heard Dad joke once, but it wasn't funny.

Mom obsessively scrolls through message boards for information about Shady's anxiety disorder, which is called selective mutism. Then she buys things she thinks might help, as if a light that changes colors or the right kind of probiotics or a special weighted blanket could somehow fix everything.

And me? I guess I mostly worry about Shady feeling left out. I've been there, and I know how lonely school can be when you're not in with the right crowd, or in with any crowd at all.

It's why I'm glad he's got Pouya. But then again, my brother's best friend isn't famous for making awesome life decisions—and whatever Pouya does, Shady does too.

And now it's 4:45.

Had Pouya decided they should play tree pirates again and gotten them both stuck at the top of an elm? Were they racing carts in the grocery-store parking lot? Unwisely trying to train baby raccoons to ride on their shoulders using cheese puffs as bait? Or, worse, were they in some kind of *real* trouble?

We live in a heritage area, with old houses and landscaped parks. But it's still part of the city. Just the other day, I saw a guy slip another guy a package behind a bench at Forest Hill Park. It could have been drugs. And our neighborhood is right next to Summerside, where Pouya and his moms live. There the sidewalks are littered with broken glass, and the mismatched curtains in the windows make the tall apartment buildings look like ratty patchwork quilts.

No matter where you live, there can be problems. For example, for the last month or so, a guy in a gorilla suit has been going around our neighborhood roaring at old ladies, throwing bananas at them, and stealing their purses. You can't make this stuff up!

Now it's 4:47.

Normally, I meet Shady and Pouya at the doors of Carleton Elementary after Environment Club, but our house had big, black ants again—the ones that pop like Rice Krispies when you squash them in a Kleenex. They were parading around the baseboards and climbing the walls. Our mom does *not* tolerate nature in the house—unless it's in the form of a tasteful flower arrangement from Blooms on Bloor.

Every time she spotted one of the ants, she shrieked and made me, Dad, or Shady squash it. But they'd reached un-squashable numbers. And the only time the exterminator could come was Friday between three thirty and six, which was why I was waiting around at home while my brother and Pouya were who-knows-where doing something defi-nitely, completely stupid.

4:49.

Finally, I caught sight of them rounding the corner onto Browning Street.

"Oh, thank God," I muttered.

"Yo, Manda." A minute later, Pou pushed the front door open casually, like he lives here—which he half does. I babysit him every day after school since his parents are busy. They emigrated from Iran about five years ago. But his Mitra-Joon is still retraining to get her pharmacy license and taking English classes, and Lili, his maman, works late. Also, they can't afford the after-school program. Anyway, I don't mind. Except for when the boys do stupid stuff.

I glared at the clock on the wall, then at my brother and his friend to make a point—not that I expected Shady to say anything. It would have gone against his rules. Rule

Number 1 being that my brother doesn't talk to—or in front of—anyone from school, and that includes his best friend.

As usual, Pouya spoke for him. "Sorry. We got delayed." He shrugged. "But it wasn't our fault."

I'd heard that one before.

"We ran into duck problems."

This was new. "Umm...*duck* problems?"

My brother bent his head so his long hair flopped over his face. He was always trying to hide behind it, but I could see through the strands that he was grinning down at his chest. That was normal in its own not-normal way. There was a story, and he wanted to tell it, but he couldn't. Not now. Later, once Pouya went home, he'd tell me all about it.

In that beat of silence, I heard water dripping against the tile floor. It was coming from Pouya's backpack—but that wasn't the only thing that was wet.

"And what happened to your pants?" I asked.

Pouya lifted one foot. He seemed surprised to find his sneaker soaked and muddy. "Oh. Well, obviously, we got wet."

He launched into an explanation about baby ducks and a daring trek across Dixon Road to reunite them with their mother.

"You did *what*?" I was talking to Pouya, but staring my brother down at the same time, because he totally should have known better.

Dixon Road has tons of traffic. Not to mention they could have gotten rabies from the ducks. Or drowned in the drainage ditch.

"Or been pecked to death by a deranged mallard," Pouya added, when I'd finished listing the reasons they were idiots.

I sighed, but I didn't see the point of making a big thing of it. Shady was home safe. Why get Mom and Dad all worked up? "Go get changed," I said. Then I looked out the still-open door behind them. "Wait a sec. Where are your bikes?" The boys were supposed to put them in the garage but never remembered. Normally, the bikes would be lying on the front path.

Shady and Pouya exchanged a look I knew well: part panicked, part guilty, and all "uh-oh, we're dead now."

"Again, it wasn't our fault," Pouya began. "We put them down on the grass for a second, and two big kids stole them."

"You've *got* to be kidding me," I said. Now there was no way around it. When Mom and Dad found out the bikes were missing—*even though I wasn't there*—it'd be all "*You're* in charge, Manda. Shady is vulnerable. We're counting on you," etc. My only hope was to control the damage.

"Okay. We'll say the bikes got stolen at school. Don't mention the ducks to any parents. But you both owe me. *Big-time*. Give me your backpacks," I ordered. "And bring down your wet clothes after you change."

Pouya started to take his backpack off but stopped after one strap. There was that "uh-oh" look passing between him and Shady again. Even guiltier and more doomed than before.

"Oh man." Pouya squinched his eyes shut.

Shady started giggling silently but maniacally. Never a good sign.

"We were running for our lives," Pouya said. "I completely forgot it was in there."

I held out one hand insistently, and Pouya handed me the backpack.

I'm not sure what I was expecting...a punctured bottle of

pop they'd been messing around with? A big wad of dripping paper towels?

I *definitely* wasn't prepared for the fluffy brown-and-yellow head that popped out when I opened the zipper.

Wak.

Wak, wak.

So, yeah. Okay. I screamed.

BUG OUT!

DISCREET SERVICE FOR ALL YOUR RESIDENTIAL PEST CONTROL NEEDS.

You don't have time for pests! Critters like ants, cockroaches, bedbugs, and more! Insects or animals that have invaded your home are more than just a nuisance. They can be irritating, embarrassing, and a threat to your property and health. Get professional service from a trusted partner in residential pest control. We'll help you regain control of your space by getting the bugs (or other pests) OUT and gone for good.

Ask us about our popular rodent special! Twenty-percent-off coupon available for referrals!

CHAPTER 3

Break and Enter

Told by Pearl Summers

I was minding my own business, walking my teacup poodle, Juliette, down Browning Street when I heard the blood-curdling scream. Imagine a violin being put through a blender set to liquefy. Not even the heavy bass line of "Get Down, Get Funky," which I was listening to on my wireless headphones, could begin to drown it out.

"Come here, muffin."

Even though Juliette had just found the perfect spot to tinkle, I scooped her up off the grass and held her tightly to my chest as I looked left and right. The source of the scream wasn't obvious at first. There was also nobody else on the street to have heard it. If someone needed rescuing, it was going to be up to me.

And that was when I noticed the suspicious white van in the driveway of Shady Cook's house.

To be clear, I'm *not* friends with Shady. I used to be, but that was a long time ago. When we were little, our moms met up most days at Forest Hill Park and walked around the edges in fast circles, swinging their arms. Some kind of fitness thing. Shady and I spent a lot time together in the sandbox, so it was impossible not to become friends, what with all the digging holes to China and selling pretend pancakes to passersby that we did.

For a while we were tight. We had a joint birthday party at the Build-A-Bear place. There were family barbecues in each other's backyards. One time our families rented a beach house together. There's a photo of us toasting marshmallows by the campfire in matching polar bear pajamas.

But that was before we started school at Carleton Elementary, when he stopped talking and became Shady. His real name's David. Shady is a nickname our kindergarten teacher, Mr. Parker, gave him because he liked to wear sunglasses everywhere, even inside.

After that, things changed. I mean, it's not easy being friends with a person who never talks. Our families still got together for barbecues, but how many times can you play charades with someone when you're the only one guessing, or Go Fish with someone who won't say "go fish"?

But just because we're not friends anymore doesn't mean I want anything tragic to happen to Shady. Obviously!

I took my headphones off. Still holding Juliette tight, I watched as a man in a blue prison jumpsuit got out of the white van in Shady's driveway and slammed the door behind him.

Juliette sensed danger. She twisted in my arms and looked straight at the man, growling low in her throat like a cell phone set to vibrate. My teacup poodle might be teddy-bear soft and small enough to fit inside a medium-size cereal bowl, but she's got killer instincts.

I ducked behind a shrub in the yard next door and watched as the guy raised his arms to stretch out a kink in his back, revealing a tattoo of a bloodred rose on his wrist. He yawned loudly, like the life of crime was wearing him out, then started to climb Shady's stairs. He knocked and waited, but there was no answer. Was he checking to make sure no one was home? It seemed likely because a few seconds later, he shrugged, then tried the knob.

My entire body tensed as he stepped inside.

Don't ask me how, but I knew: it was the Banana Bandit—the weird guy who'd been disguising himself as a gorilla and snatching old ladies' purses. Sure, the man wasn't wearing his gorilla suit—but that didn't mean much. He must have gotten caught. The police probably confiscated the suit when they put him in jail. Obviously, he'd escaped, and now he was on the run, looking for places to hide and houses to rob. Why had he picked Shady's place? Who knew! I mean, why did he throw bananas at old ladies? The guy was a nutjob.

Then I had an even more sickening thought. Shady's parents' cars weren't in the driveway. Did that mean he was home alone? If he was, would he even be able to call the police? *Could* Shady scream for help? Maybe...I reasoned... if he was terrified enough.

Either way, a break-in would be too much for a kid like Shady to handle. Friends or not, if I didn't step in, I knew he was doomed.

The front door slammed shut behind the bandit. I had

to act fast. I could already picture the newspaper headlines: "Brave Nine-Year-Old Girl Saves Neighbor in Distress." Or maybe: "Banana Bandit Captured by Gutsy Girl and Plucky Poodle." It wasn't my main motivation—obviously—but it was going to look nice in my scrapbook. Or maybe framed in the hallway.

"Come on, Juliette," I said, trying to sound braver than I felt for her sake.

I ran across the lawn and pushed Shady's door open, hoping to gain the element of surprise.

That part worked.

"Ow! Watch it, would ya?" the bandit roared as the door hit him in the back.

"Quick! Close the door! Don't let him get out!"

It was Shady's sister, Amanda—or Manda, for short. She used to babysit me sometimes: we'd play ponies, and she'd French braid my hair and let me try on her jewelry. But now that she was in high school she'd gone goth, with black eyeliner, black clothes, and ugly army boots. Not only was she older than me, but she looked way scarier. I don't know why she expected me to be the one to stop the bandit, but again, I acted out of selfless instinct.

"Turn yourself in!" I yelled at the Banana Bandit in my loudest voice. "Or I'll sic my dog on you!"

The guy looked at Juliette and *laughed*! Talk about rude!

"Not him!" Manda said. "*Him!*" She pointed at the floor.

Shady was there, crawling along after a duckling who seemed to be making a break for it. Just before Shady could wrap his hands around the little duck, it swerved left after a big, black ant it was chasing.

"Calm down, okay? You're all freaking him out!"

It was Pouya. Shady's best/only friend—and the other big reason I will never hang out with Shady Cook again. The word *annoying* doesn't even begin to describe Pouya Fard. I have to sit behind him in class, so I'd know. He's always making weird clicking noises with his mouth or backing his chair into my desk on purpose while yelling "Earthquake!" Once, I watched him eat a booger. A big, gooey one.

Also, if you can believe this, when he started at our school back in kindergarten, he didn't know how to climb stairs. He scooched up and down on his butt to get to the library. Mr. Parker said it was because they didn't have stairs in the refugee camp where he'd been living, so he was still learning, but seriously, it's not that hard! I'm ninety percent sure he was only doing it for attention, which is why he does everything.

And then there's his name. If your name was Pouya Fard, wouldn't you at least try to change it? I mean, hello! *Someone* is going to call you Poo Fart.

Oh, and did I mention that he's rude? For example, at that moment, he said, "What are *you* doing here?" and made a ghoul face at me. Shady—his number one fan—giggled silently before going back to duckling chasing.

Unfortunately, I didn't get the chance to point out that it *wasn't* Pouya's house, and he didn't have the right to ask me that—because Juliette caught sight of the duckling.

Ruuuuuf. Ruuuuuf. Ruf. Ruf, ruf, ruf.

My dog has a thing for ducks. It's why we can't walk her near the ravine anymore. Her whole body started to twist like a boiling noodle. Before I knew it, she'd wriggled out of my arms and launched herself through the air.

Ruf. Ruf, ruf, ruf.

Wak. WAK, WAK, WAK!

The duckling's webbed feet floundered against the shiny tile floor, and if it wasn't for the fact that it started flapping its wings and getting some lift, it would have been a duck-flavored dog treat for sure.

"Juliette!" I called. "Stop." But even though she'd won "best behaved" in her puppy class, all her training went straight out the window. She growled, then she lunged.

Shady only just managed to swoop in to grab the duckling in time. For once, he *wasn't* wearing his dumb mirrored sunglasses, and he glared out at me from under his floppy hair.

"Get your stupid dog out of here, Pearl," Pouya yelled. As if by selflessly trying to stop a robbery in progress, I was the one who'd done something wrong. Like I could have known in a million thousand years that there would randomly be a baby duck in Shady's house!

Well, fine! If I wasn't needed or appreciated! I picked up the yapping Juliette and tucked her under my arm. "Come on, Julie-woolie-doggy-woggy," I said, trying to soothe her with her favorite nickname, but it didn't work.

"Look. Do you want me to take care of the ants or not?" the man in the jumpsuit yelled to Manda, over the barking.

That was when I noticed the label on his suit—which, in my defense, looked exactly like a prison uniform. *Bug Out! Pest Control.* Such an easy mistake.

"Yes, do the ants. But can you help us with the duck first?" Manda pleaded. "You trap squirrels and raccoons, right? If you have a cage we can put it in, I'm sure my parents will pay you extra."

But the man started talking about things like liability and work orders. I don't know exactly, because I wasn't really listening. I had my hands full with Juliette, and nobody was even bothering to open the front door to help me.

Pouya was pulling wet books out of his backpack.

Shady was cradling the duckling in his arm and rocking back and forth with it like it was a baby.

"It's not that I don't want to help," the man concluded. "I would if I could, but I'm not licensed for duck removal."

Juliette had finally stopped barking, but she was still whimpering.

"Well, can you at least tell me who to call?" Manda said. "Because my mom's going to freak out if she comes home to find—"

All of a sudden, she stopped.

I followed her gaze.

So did Pouya.

"Shhhhhhh. Shhhhhh." Shady was looking down, stroking the duckling's back gently. It had nestled its tiny beak into his armpit.

Like I said, Shady and I used to be friends. He'd always been kind of quiet, but there was a time when he'd talk to me. At least to tell me what outfit he wanted for his Build-A-Bear and whether or not he was putting pretend blueberries in his sand pancakes—but that was a long time ago.

"Shhhh. Shhhhhhh. Quack, quack."

These days, he doesn't answer in class or talk to kids at recess or do read-alouds. If anyone asks him a question, he looks straight ahead like he can't hear them. He doesn't even laugh out loud. For the last five years, he'd been completely silent.

"Shhhhh. Quack, quack."

Until now.

THE MOBILE ANIMAL CLINIC

Specializing in backyard chickens and wounded wildlife

INVOICE FOR PROFESSIONAL SERVICES PROVIDED

Dr. Nancy Jacobi
352 Peacelily Crescent
VET REGISTRATION NUMBER: 10000027
DATE: May 30
TRANSACTION NUMBER: 5155041
PATIENT: Sven (duckling)

Record of Services Provided

Standard Exam:	$ 85.00
Consultation:	$ 35.00
Subtotal:	$120.00
Sales Tax @ 6.5%	$ 7.80
TOTAL:	$127.80
PAID:	$127.80

---

*The Mobile Animal Clinic thanks you
very much for your business!*

CHAPTER 4

Emotional Support Duck

Told by Manda

My brother decided to call the duckling Sven…but the name didn't work out. Actually, a lot of things about the duckling didn't work out at first.

The most obvious problem was Mom. Not surprising. We're talking about a person who screams when she sees an ant. As I predicted, she lost her mind when she got home from work and first saw the duckling—even though by then I'd made Shady and Pouya put it in a cardboard box and take it outside.

Mom wouldn't go near the box. Like she was afraid the duckling might flap up and peck off her nose. And okay—

I'll admit that at first, I'd been scared of it too…but once it wasn't popping out of a backpack and giving me a heart attack, it was completely harmless and totally cute.

When Pou's maman, Lili, came to pick him up, she summed it up perfectly as she reached into the box and gently stroked the duckling's head. "Hello there, little one. Aren't you all that's good in the world?"

Sven stole everyone's heart like that, right from the start. Everyone's except Mom's. She said Shady and Dad had to take the duckling back on their way to Shady's therapy appointment—end of story. But when Dad and Shady got to Dixon Creek, the mother duck turned her back on Sven, who I guess already smelled too much like humans. And when Dad told Dr. Nugget how Shady had made sounds out loud in front of people outside our family for the first time in years, the therapist had an idea.

"An *emotional support duck*?" Shady and I heard the crash of a pot or pan hitting the stove. "Is this the kind of garbage we pay him a hundred and eighty dollars an hour for?" Mom said.

Shady glanced toward the heating vent, which was carrying sound from the kitchen to the basement bathroom. The duckling had been banished there as soon as they got home from therapy. I could see the worry all over my brother's face, so I tried to distract him.

"Look!" I started lining frozen peas up along the side of the tub, where we'd made the duckling a shallow lake. It scrambled up the side to grab each one, slipping back down every time with a splash.

Upstairs, Dad was saying something, but his voice was too low and even to make out.

"Do you think Dad can talk her into letting me keep him?" Shady asked. His voice came out a little scratchy, since it was one of the first things he'd said out loud in hours. (He never talks to Dr. Nugget. I guess they just stare at each other for an hour?) "Maybe if I promise to do everything the duck needs and take care of him completely?" he went on hopefully.

I know. Shady talking—just like that—it's strange, but that's how it is. At school, at the doctor's office, when our grandparents visit from Vermont: Shady doesn't make a sound or say a single word. But when it's just him and me, or my parents—when he's completely comfortable—he talks as easily as any other kid.

The fact that he *can* talk makes his *not talking* all the more confusing to people. Some of our relatives even take it personally, but I know it's not a choice. I tried not talking for a whole day once, but I barely made it to ten in the morning. It was like holding my breath, only my thoughts were the trapped air needing to burst out. *Nobody* would choose to live like that on purpose, day after day.

"I'd even take him on little ducky walks around the block and tuck him into bed at night."

"Right," I said. "Because Mom would be all about letting a duck use the good linens."

And here's one more thing that people might be surprised to know about my brother. Underneath all that anxiety, he's got a wicked sense of humor and a way with words. For example:

"I'd call him my little splashy-washy-ducky-wucky." Shady flipped his hair off his face, Pearl Summers style. He looked up and grinned at me, then fed Sven another pea. "Isn't that right, my sweetie-wheety-webby-feety? Are you my bitty-whittle teacup duck?"

I laughed out loud. I couldn't help it. Ever since Pearl Summers had been mean enough to uninvite Shady to her

seventh birthday party (because, in her words "We're playing the telephone game, so…"), making fun of her in private
had been one of my and Shady's things. Laughing at her
pom-pom-on-a-string of a dog made us feel a little better
too. I mean, they were both a lot to take.

I'd know. I used to babysit Pearl when she was in first
and second grade. She once tried to convince me that she
was actual royalty because she had a two-level, castle-style
princess bed in her room. I'm pretty sure she seriously
believed it. But like, no, honey. That just means your parents
spoil you rotten, so now you think you're better than
everyone.

"I'd even pay the vet bills," Shady offered. "Out of my
allowance. They *might* say yes."

"They might." I didn't want to be the one to disappoint
him. "It's not impossible." I looked at Sven sadly. Shady did
the same. I think we both knew it was never going to happen.

I'd spent my entire life begging for a kitten or a puppy.
In fifth grade, I won a black swish-tailed fish at Meghan's
birthday party. I named her Hepburn. Mom and Dad made
me give her right back. So, a duck? *A wild animal?* No way.

As if to confirm it, Mom's voice came through the vent

again. "Where's the research?" Another pot slammed upstairs. "It's insane. Plus, it'd be just one more thing to make
other kids think he's weird. Did Dr. Nugget even think of
that?"

The basement bathroom has spiders. Mom never uses it.
Obviously, she didn't know about the vent and how easy it
was to hear conversations in the kitchen. Still, I hated her
a little bit for what she'd just said. And the fact that it was
true didn't make it any less awful. Actually, just the opposite.

I closed the air stopper on the vent. "It's too hot in here
anyway," I said, being careful not to look Shady in the eye.
Then I had an idea. "I wonder if he can catch them." I threw
a few peas toward the duck. The first three splashed into
the water, but once I sort of arched the peas up high enough,
Sven spotted them in time and was able to gobble them
right out of midair.

Before long, the duckling was catching every single one—
even if it had to race from one end of the bathtub to the
other to do it.

"Here, Sven!"

Shady tossed a few more peas. He was grinning and his
eyes were bright, which made me almost regret throwing

the peas in the first place. The more attached he got, the worse it was going to be when Mom and Dad sent the duckling away.

"Guys! Dinner!" Dad's voice came from the top of the stairs.

"Come on," I said. But instead of getting up to follow me, Shady leaned over the edge of the bathtub, holding out his hand. The duckling swam over and rubbed the top of its head against Shady's palm.

"What if he gets scared while we're eating?" Shady asked. "I bet he's never been alone before."

"He'll be okay," I said. But no matter how I tried to reassure him—by saying we'd leave the light on, by putting on music from my phone to keep the duck company, by promising Shady dinner would only take ten minutes if he ate fast—my brother wouldn't budge from the bathroom floor. And when Shady decides to be stubborn, his stubbornness is legendary.

"Dinner!" Dad called again, louder. "Now."

I went up alone. "I can't get him out. You try."

But Mom and I were nearly done with our Salisbury steak pies when Dad came back to the table, alone.

"Leave him!" he said when my mom started to get up to try dealing with the situation. "He'll come up when he gets hungry enough."

Mom didn't look happy, but there's a certain tone my dad gets sometimes that you just don't argue with, even if you're my mom.

Anyway, Dad changed the subject.

"So, Manda…" he started. "I saw Oscar Lebretton at a lunch and learn today. You know, Matthew's dad?"

I knew Matthew Lebretton. Vagueishly. He'd sat in front of me in math the year before. He wore a leather jacket, even in the summer.

"Apparently he just joined a film club at school. His dad says they're studying the classics—like *Citizen Kane* and *Breakfast at Tiffany's*. They're working up to making films to enter into some kind of contest."

I knew all about it. Ever since I'd watched the 1939 version of *The Wizard of Oz* with my uncle at a rerun cinema, I've been addicted to old films. There's something so clean and classy about them. Like, who needs to sit through two hours of explosions and cheesy dialogue when you can get the same drama from a single longing look between Clark

Gable and Vivien Leigh in *Gone with the Wind*?

Mr. Maloney started the Film Fanatics club because of a contest from the National Film Society. There was going to be a weeklong international student cinema fest in New Orleans next year, and rumor had it the winner got to go— all expenses paid. A bunch of kids at school were already desperate to win, including my friends Carly and Beth. Not because they cared about cinema. They were mostly in it for the free trip. And (probably because they figured I could help them win), they'd been trying to talk me into joining with them. But, as cool as it sounded, I knew I couldn't. And, honestly, I didn't really want to anyway. I wasn't a school club person.

"Why don't you sign up?" Dad said. "You love old films."

"I don't know. They meet after school, so..." I took a sip of milk.

"So...what's the problem?" Dad asked, but all it took was a look from Mom across the table to remind him what the problem was.

"We could ask Angie Murray to watch Shady and Pouya," Dad said. "How often does the film club meet? Once a week? Didn't Angie just do her babysitting course?"

Angie Murray lives two houses down. Her voice is so loud that she practically yells when she talks, and once, at a neighborhood garage sale, I'd caught her teasing Shady by trying to make him talk into some old walkie-talkies and then pretending they were broken.

Luckily, Mom didn't even consider it.

"I don't think Shady's ready for that quite yet," she said.

"Well, I don't accept that," Dad answered.

"Excuse me?" Mom tried to level him with a look.

"How is Shady supposed to get ready if we don't push him?"

"Dr. Nugget specifically said we shouldn't try to force him into new situations," Mom countered.

"And Dr. Nugget also specifically said we should let him keep that duck. So you're going to pick and choose from his advice now?"

Mom was boiling. I could almost see the steam coming out her nose holes.

"It's okay." I hated it when they argued. "I don't really want to join anyway. I can just watch movies at home. It's no big deal."

And it really wasn't. Shady was more important. School

was a nightmare for my brother. Except for Pouya, kids ignored him or, worse, teased him—especially after he'd wet his pants at the beginning of fourth grade. His teacher had insisted that Shady had to make some kind of hand signal if he wanted permission to go use the bathroom, and he had been too scared to do it. You'd think signaling his teacher would be no big deal, but it breaks Rule Number 2, which is that he does everything he can not to call attention to himself. Although, in this case, it totally backfired. Just try wetting your pants in fourth grade without everyone noticing.

By the time he got home, Shady needed someone he could trust and talk to, and I was one of his only options. I wasn't going to abandon him with Angie Murray. And even if I *did* join Film Fanatics...and on the off chance I *did* win the trip, there was no way I could leave him for a week to go to New Orleans. So what was the point of signing up?

Dad had his eyes locked on Mom. "Look. All I'm saying is, the things we've been doing aren't working. So maybe it's time to try something new." He turned to me. "You're joining that club, Manda. I'll write you a check for the registration fee after dinner."

Mom glared at Dad across the table.

"Manda, if you're finished, would you go upstairs?" Her voice was balanced on a thin edge between anger and tears.

I nodded and cleared my plate.

It took hours, and there were raised voices. It was already past Shady's bedtime when Dad came and got me. He asked me to come down to the basement, where Mom was waiting outside the bathroom door.

Dad knocked, then went in, but Mom stayed a safe distance back. Sven was out of the tub now, curled in my brother's lap in a towel, fast asleep. I could tell from Shady's eyes that he'd been crying.

"We've agreed to try keeping the duck," Mom said. At those words, my brother's face lit up. "Provided it's healthy and doesn't cause problems," she went on. "It needs to be checked by a vet. And it stays outside or down here in the bathroom."

Shady stood up and handed me the swaddled duckling, then stepped past Dad and threw his arms around Mom. *Thank you* is one of the things he just can't seem to say— even to us—but the message was there in his arms. "I'll take such good care of him," he said instead. "You won't have to worry about anything."

"And, Manda, we'll try having Angie babysit Shady and Pouya once a week so you can join the film club," Mom said.

At that, my brother shot me a panicked look, and I shot one right back, but in the end, his happiness about the duck seemed to outweigh his worry about Angie. Maybe mine did, too, because with the duckling now nestled in my arms, I felt calmer than I would have expected about the whole thing.

Mom sighed. "Now come and get ready for bed. Both of you. It's getting late."

The next afternoon, a lady with a long, gray braid stopped by. She was a wildlife specialist from a mobile animal clinic that Dad found online. She went to the basement bathroom to see Sven, and when she came back up, she pronounced the duckling healthy and told us how to look after it.

"No bread," she said. "Bread is very bad for ducks. Lots of veggies, like the frozen peas you've got downstairs. Corn is good too. No citrus fruit. And you'll need to pick up some special feed called duck crumble. You can buy it from a farm-supply store or order it for her online."

Shady, who'd been taking notes, looked up. The question was in his furrowed eyebrows.

"*Her?*" I asked.

"It's a female duckling."

And that was how we ended up with our first family pet—which wasn't a pet, exactly. She was a service animal. An "emotional support duck." And her new name was Svenrietta.

COME ONE, COME ALL
TO THE
Carleton Elementary School Sock Ball!

Are you ready to dance, dance, dance, have the time of your life, and make a difference for someone less fortunate?

Did you know that socks are the number one most requested item from homeless shelters? On Wednesday, December 3, at first period, we're having a sock ball!

DJ Doozy will be spinning tunes in the gym while we have a massive indoor snowball fight using balled-up socks that will then be collected for donation to Harbor House. There will even be an awesome prize. You'll get one chance to win it for every pair of clean, new socks. Don't leave home without your sock donations and your dancing shoes!

It's going to be amazing!

See you there!

Sincerely,

Pearl Summers (your student council president)

CHAPTER 5

A Duck at School

Told by Pouya

Right from the start, Svenrietta was more than your average duck.

I never thought Shady would get to keep her, but he told me the news first thing at school on Monday.

He started by pointing at the ground in front of him.

"Sidewalk?" I guessed.

He bent his arms inward and flapped his elbows.

"Chicken?"

He shook his head, pointed at the ground again, and when that didn't work, he cradled his arms across his chest and rocked them back and forth.

"Oh! The baby duck!"

He pointed down again as if to say *here* and *now*.

"You still have it?"

He grinned. Nodded hard. It was the most excited I'd ever seen my best friend. Even the time we traded his dad's lawn mower to an old guy down the street for a real, working go-kart, Shady hadn't been this pumped.

I asked questions all day, but it was hard for him to explain. I only found out the details later.

Basically, Svenrietta was a duck with a job—in charge of helping Shady feel better. Less freaked out about stuff. And she was really, really good at it.

Her main duty was to go places with him. Like out for ice cream, to his therapy appointments, and even to the grocery store.

She learned to walk on a leash with a special harness, and she was better behaved than some dogs I'd met. Not only that, but Shady managed to train her, because she'd do just about anything for the green peas he kept in his pocket. When Shady closed his hand into a fist, she had learned to sit. When he opened it and tilted his palm upward, she got up. He only had to clap twice for "come here," and she'd come booping across the room to him, wiggling her fuzzy butt.

The only thing she didn't do on command was poop. Ducks are constant poopers, so she had to wear special duck diapers that Shady's mom ordered online. Svenrietta's diapers had different patterns: hearts, stars, even ones with tiny skulls for the days she wanted to look tough. Shady had to change them, and it was gross, but he didn't mind. That's how much he loved her.

Actually, before long, *everyone* loved her. Even Shady's mom. You could tell because she kept a special certificate from Shady's psychiatrist in her purse and threatened to report people—like the guy at the pizza place, or the taxi driver who claimed to have a "no ducks in my cab" rule—if they wouldn't let Svenrietta go wherever Shady went.

Shady's mom is the kind of lady who gets things dry-cleaned and wears a real diamond necklace. She expects things to be the way she expects them. Everyone—including the taxi driver—gave in quick. Everyone except our principal, Mrs. Mackie, who said a duck would disrupt the learning environment. *That* didn't fly with Shady's mom. She went straight to the school board office, then she called a lawyer.

It took a while. We spent our summer afternoons watching Svenrietta paddle around in Shady's old kiddie pool in his backyard and teaching her tricks for peas. The fall of fifth grade started. Shady wore a pair of ripped overalls and tucked Svenri under one arm for the world's easiest and most legit farmer's costume that Halloween. The first snow fell, and Shady's mom ordered a pair of special duck boots so Svenrietta could walk in the snow.

She'd grown from a fluff-poof into an almost full-size duck—but, finally, at the beginning of December, Svenrietta was allowed to start school on probation. That meant she could come, but if she was too distracting to the other kids, she'd get banned.

Wednesday, December 3, was her first day. It was good timing, because I needed some cheering up.

"Hey," I said dully when I met Shady in front of the school that day. He was getting out of his dad's car. "You got her?"

Shady gave me the A-OK nod.

He was carrying Svenrietta in a special sling, tucked inside his coat to keep her warm. From certain angles, it made him look like a pregnant lady.

He must have noticed the dead tone of my voice because

he raised his eyebrows like *You okay?*

"Have you seen this?" I pulled a folded-up piece of newsprint out of my pocket.

He read the headline. Bit his lip. Shook his head sadly.

I sighed heavily in response.

What were we so bummed about? Oh, nothing really. *Just the end of the world.*

According to internet sources, Planet Q—also known as the planet Quaninbar—was hurtling toward us at a speed of 1,000 light years per hour. Astral-science experts theorized that it would make contact with Earth at the stroke of midnight on New Year's Day, probably blasting us all to smithereens.

The whole thing was spelled out in an ancient Mayan prophecy. When I'd heard about it two months before, I hadn't exactly believed it, but the first three signs had already come to pass.

First: *The sea will turn black, and many living things will die.*

There was a huge oil spill in the Gulf of Mexico a month ago. They showed pictures on the news of dead birds washed up on shore and volunteers cleaning sea turtles with toothbrushes.

And, okay. Oil spills happen. But, two weeks later: *An unholy racket will rattle the skies.* Fireworks went off for no reason what sounded like a few blocks away. It wasn't even a holiday! The windows in our apartment building shook for almost an hour.

Then, just that morning, I'd nearly choked on my cereal when page four of the world news section reported that in Wyoming, a sinkhole the size of an Olympic swimming pool had opened up in a highway, and a van carrying puppies to a local shelter fell right in. The third sign, clear as day: *A crater will open and swallow the innocent.* What could be more innocent than puppies?

There were only two signs to go, which made it official: the human race had about four weeks left before Planet Q struck on New Year's Day. That was less than 28 days... about 665 hours. The clock was ticking—and the worst part was, most people didn't even care.

"Come on," I said to Shady, because the first bell had already rung. "Let's go line up before Svenri gets cold."

"Yo, Gavin!" I said, once we were in line. "Have you seen this?" I held up the newspaper article. "It's like I told you! The end is near."

Gavin, who's one of the smartest kids in our class, glanced up from the book he was reading. He sighed. "Are you still talking about Planet Q?" he asked. "It's a total hoax. You know that, right?"

"*Is it?*" I pressed the article closer to his face. I pointed to the part about puppies, but he didn't seem impressed, so I tried Wendel Munch. "It's the third sign," I said, showing him the article.

"Oh shut up, Pou," he answered, turning back to face the front of the line.

Then Pearl Summers got in on tearing me down. "Nobody believes you, okay?" She glared at me. "It's what happens when every second thing you say is a lie."

"Yeah," her friend Monica agreed. "Like, we all know your uncle didn't really invent crackers."

Okay, yes. That was something I made up one day to be funny, but was it that impossible to believe? *Someone* invented crackers. Why not my uncle?

"Fine!" I threw my hands up and turned to Shady. "See if I come to their rescue when the next sign comes to pass, and winged machines start falling from the sky."

The second bell rang, and we all filed in.

"Good morning, Shady!" Pearl Summers cooed, once we'd stopped in front of the coat hooks. I wouldn't have thought it was possible, but since that day in Shady's front hall when we'd first brought Svenri home, Pearl had upped her annoyingness. Over the last few months, she'd gotten meaner and meaner, especially when her friends were around to impress. (The week before, she'd asked DuShawn, a boy in our class who has long hair and likes to wear dresses sometimes, if she could borrow his outfit, then laughed out loud with Monica and Rebecca when he said yes.) And, I swear, she purposely walked past Shady's house with her prancy little hamster-sized dog every day, just so that it could yap at Svenrietta. And now this routine...

"Yeah. *Good morning, Shady!*" Pearl's friend Rebecca echoed.

"Would you *stop* doing that?" I yelled it straight into their faces because, like I said, I was in *no* mood. "You know he hates it."

At least, Pearl *should* have known it. She used to be Shady's best friend. Their families had rented mansions on the beach together and stuff when they were little. Shady showed me a picture of them at some kind of fair, grinning with pink and blue teeth while they ate sticks of cotton candy that were bigger than their heads. She knew his deal. But since she'd started hanging out with Rebecca and Monica, she liked to act as if she didn't.

"Okay. First of all, we weren't talking to you, Pou." Pearl wrinkled her nose like my name smelled. "And second, saying good morning is the polite thing to do."

Is it though?

Pearl knew Shady wasn't going to answer. She knew it made him squirm when people talked right at him. And still, she and her stupid friends did this every day, like it was a project. Like if they just kept chipping away, they could extract words from him.

Or maybe they were just trying to make a point that they were better people than him because they said it and he didn't say it back.

I didn't know exactly. Just trust me. It was the meanest kind of good morning, and I was done with it. That's why I stomped on Rebecca's foot. Not hard. And she was wearing snow boots. It couldn't have hurt that much, but first she screamed like a baby and then she shoved me, sending me flying straight into Shady.

"Watch it!" I yelled after I'd found my balance.

"Yeah. Careful, Rebecca," Pearl sneered. "If you bump into Shady too hard, he might pee himself."

"That's not what I meant," I yelled. "He's got his duck inside his coat. You could have squashed her."

"Oh whatever, Pou." Rebecca rolled her eyes.

"Yeah. Stop lying," Pearl added.

I'd been telling people for weeks that Svenrietta would be coming to school soon, but they acted like I was making it up. And even though Pearl knew it was true, she was acting like it was a lie just to annoy me.

Finally, I had a chance to prove myself.

"Does this look like a lie?" I reached over and unzipped Shady's coat.

Svenrietta poked her head out of the sling.

Wak.

Both girls screamed.

"Oh my God!" Shushanna said, catching sight of Svenri from across the hall. "Shady has a duck!"

"Awwww! That's so cute!" her friend Sara squealed.

"Okay, everyone. Into class." Our teacher, Mrs. Okah, managed to break up the crowd that had started to gather around Shady and Svenrietta, but as soon as we got into Room 9, the uproar started again.

"Can I pet it?"

"What's its name?"

"Mrs. Okah, that's so unfair! Why's he allowed to bring a pet to school? Can I bring my cat?"

Mrs. Okah had to raise one hand and do her shoosh face. When that didn't work, she switched off the lights.

"We'll talk about Shady's duck after announcements, before we head to the gym for the Sock Ball," she promised.

All through the national anthem, Shady ground his heels into the floor nervously. Then, while Principal Mackie made announcements about Environment Club and the Sock Ball, Shady scribbled furiously on a piece of scrap paper that looked like a crumpled-up flyer. It's something he always does in class when he's nervous—but he was scribbling harder than ever.

When the announcements ended, Pearl and her friends Rebecca and Monica left to go decorate the gym for the dance, since they're on student council. That meant three of Shady's least favorite people were gone. Still, I could tell by his hunched-up shoulders that he was scared to talk about the duck, and that he didn't like the way everyone was staring at him.

But a strange thing happened.

"As you've noticed," Mrs. Okah said. "We have a new class member. This is Shady's emotional support duck. Her name is Svenrietta."

After that, Mrs. Okah went over basic duck rules. Stuff like "You can only touch her if Shady agrees," "Do not feed her anything, ever," and "She's a service animal. Not a pet." But once that was done, kids had tons of questions—and they *weren't* ones Mrs. Okah knew the answers to.

"Where did you get her?" Shushanna asked.

I jumped in to tell the story before Shady had to worry about it.

"We took her home from Dixon Creek kind of by accident. Then her mother wouldn't take her back. She was all like—" I flapped my arms and did my best angry duck impression, and some of the kids laughed.

"What does she eat?"

"Mainly special duck food, but she also likes veggies."

While I explained how, even though lots of people feed ducks bread, it's bad for them, Shady reached into the sling and pulled Svenrietta out. She quacked and shook her feathers, sending out little puffs of fluff, then settled onto his lap.

"Oh my goodness! Aweeeee!" Shushanna squealed.

"She's the cutest thing I've ever seen." Tanya leaned across her desk to see better.

I glanced over at Shady, expecting him to be cringing under the attention, but he was actually smiling. Not a lot. It was a pinched kind of smile. But still.

"Is she wearing a diaper?" Mohammed asked with a little snort.

Shady nodded.

That might not sound like a huge deal, but it was. Shady doesn't usually use actions to talk to other kids at school— just to me, and it took about a year after we met before he even started doing that.

"Does she always have to wear it?"

He nodded again.

Mrs. Okah was trying not to let the surprise about Shady's nods show on her face, but she wasn't doing a great job of it.

"Okay," she said. "Just a few more questions for Shady,

and then I want to go over last night's math before the Sock Ball starts."

Kathryn wanted to know if the duck could fly.

"She can, but she doesn't like to," I answered. "She always wants to stick near Shady, since he's her mom."

Linn—one of the English as a Second Language students—asked if the duck liked to do water. Connor laughed and repeated it like she'd said something dirty, "*Do* water," but I glared at him. She was obviously just trying to ask if Svenri liked to swim. Next, Andrew asked what her favorite food was.

Shady kept answering the questions that needed a yes or no, and I handled the rest. In the end, there were *way* more than just a few, but Mrs. Okah couldn't get the class to settle down, so she let them keep asking.

"Can I have your attention, please." Mrs. Mackie's voice came over the PA. "All students in grades four to five should head to the gym for the Sock Ball now."

That was when Shady and I got mobbed.

"Can I try holding her?" asked Carolyn Richards, who'd never talked to me before unless it was to say something like, "Ew. What's that mushy stuff in your lunch?"

I consulted Shady, who gave a half nod with a little shrug.

"Maybe," I translated. "Ask us later, at recess."

"Is it okay if I pet her?"

"Me too?"

Shady nodded.

"One at a time. This isn't a petting zoo. All right. Enough," I said, after at least ten hands had reached out to stroke Svenri.

We started for the gym with a fan club of kids watching the duck waddle down the hall in her happy-face diaper.

Us! With a fan club! Shady, who nobody ever paid attention to unless it was to tease him about not talking or that time he peed his pants, and me, who usually just got on people's nerves.

You know, my maman and Mitra-Joon always say the best way to get people to like you is to "just be your wonderful self."

Turns out that's a huge lie.

The *actual* best way to get people to like you is to bring a duck to school.

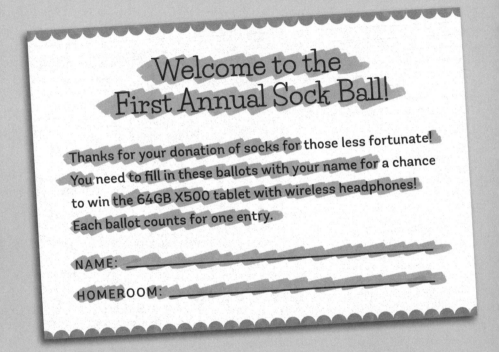

Welcome to the First Annual Sock Ball!

Thanks for your donation of socks for those less fortunate! You need to fill in these ballots with your name for a chance to win the 64GB X500 tablet with wireless headphones! Each ballot counts for one entry.

NAME: _____

HOMEROOM: _____

CHAPTER 6

The Suck Ball

Told by Pearl Summers

"Oh my God! No!"

There were mere minutes to go before the Sock Ball started, and I was *FREAKING OUT*. The gym walls were covered in sparkling snowflakes—each one painstakingly hand-cut from glittery paper. Twinkle lights cast an inviting glow from the stage, where DJ Doozy was ready to spin a carefully selected playlist of tunes, and blue and white streamers draped the entrance to create a magical wintry welcome. Then Tamille and Arjana unfurled the banner that had been their one and only responsibility as members of the Sock Ball committee.

"We are *not* hanging that up," I said.

There was a hush in the gym. Tamille seemed like she might cry.

"It says '*Suck* Ball'!" I looked to my friends Rebecca and Monica for support. They were both wincing.

"Yes," Tamille said, but her accent made it sound like *yass*. "We make it just like you said. Welcome to the suck ball."

"Sock. Saaaaahck." I stretched out the sound so she'd get it. She didn't.

"Suuuuuuuhck," she repeated.

And that's what you get when you put ESL students in charge of the banner. Mrs. Carlisle, the teacher supervisor, should have known better.

"We can fix it," Marco Saunders, one of the only guy members of the committee said. "Just round out the *U* into an *O*."

I sighed. Leave it to a boy to think a quick fix like that would work. We'd never find a marker that perfectly matched that shade of aqua. It would look terrible.

"Just hang it at the very back of the gym," I ordered. Maybe no one would notice.

Anyway, it wasn't the most important thing. The most

important thing was that Connor was almost definitely going to ask me to dance. Well, that and the fact that we were going to collect a ton of socks for poor people. Obviously.

"Where's the ballot box?" I shouted in a panic.

"Rebecca just went to get it," Monica answered over her shoulder. She was already walking to the back of the gym to hang the banner.

"And the confetti cannons?"

"Ready to go."

Thank God for Rebecca and Monica. Being student council president is a huge responsibility. There's no way I could do it without smart, dependable friends by my side.

"How do you want for us to help?" Tamille had sidled up to me—like I didn't already have my hands full enough without having to find jobs for the least helpful helpers!

"Why don't you and Arjana walk down the hall and welcome people, okay?" I suggested. It was the simplest thing I could think of. "Say 'Welcome to the *Sock* Ball.' Actually…" I thought better of it. "Just say 'Welcome to the *winter dance.*'"

Already, I could see my class coming toward the gym—

walking slower than I would have liked. They were all crowded around Shady, Pou, and the stupid duck, which was waddling along at a snail's pace. On the bright side, at least it gave me a minute to get ready.

I freshened my lip balm. "Places, everyone!" I hollered, as Rebecca ran to the table with the ballot box. "Dim the lights! Start the music!" I yelled to DJ Doozy—a potbellied guy in a glittery vest who my dad had hired as a donation to the school. The opening drumbeat of "Shake It, Shake It" started up. The biggest event of the school year was about to begin.

"Welcome to the Sock Ball!" I said with a big smile, once my class had finally gotten close enough to hear me over the music. "Please get your socks ready for counting. For each pair you donate, you'll get a ballot for the drawing to win the X500 tablet computer."

Not to brag, but the tablet was a big deal, and it was all thanks to me. My dad's friend Gary works in the head office at Best Buy. I'd personally asked him for the donation, and the tablet he gave us was top-of-the-line, with 64 gigabytes of RAM and wireless headphones. Kids had been going nuts talking about how much they wanted it—and based on the overstuffed plastic bags of socks they were carrying, most of them were in it to win it. Of course, there were a few exceptions.

Jasmin brought fifteen pairs. Mark had twenty-eight. Then Aisha stepped up to the table.

"Two pairs of socks," I said, giving her a small smile as I counted out two ballots for her. "Great effort."

I meant it sincerely. She never brought in cupcakes for class celebrations or even dressed up for Halloween. For Aisha, it *was* a great effort...but she totally twisted my words.

"It's not my fault," she said. "That's all my mom bought."

"No big deal." It was Connor Johnson, standing behind her. Even from the other side of the table, he smelled *amazing*—like the ocean on a rainy day. I think he might have borrowed a few sprays of his dad's cologne. "More chances for me to win."

Connor held up his bag, then raised a second one—both stuffed full. Had he really made all that effort just to win the tablet, or was it partly to impress me?

I smiled. "That's so awesome, Connor," I said. "You'll definitely have a great chance."

"Hold up. Wait a second." Pou stepped out from behind Connor. His voice made me cringe. "So the more socks your family can afford to buy, the better chance you have of winning? Mrs. Okah, that's completely unfair," he complained to our teacher. She was busy telling Mike and Hassan to stop playing with the water fountain, though, so she didn't pay him much attention—not that she would have anyway. Pouya is always complaining about something or lying about something or making trouble or annoying people.

"It's completely fair!" I pointed out. "And anyway, it's not like socks are hard to get. You can buy them at the dollar store."

Marco and I each took one of Connor's bags and started counting. "I got thirty-three," I said.

"Twenty-five," he reported.

A grand total of fifty-eight! The highest number yet.

Pouya kept muttering about unfairness, but I ignored it. When he stepped up to the table, it was so obvious that he was only making a thing about it because he'd brought three pairs.

"Keep that thing on its leash!" I said to Shady as he and Pou walked past with the ridiculous duck.

The other fifth graders came next, and then two classes of fourth graders. By the time we'd counted the last of the socks and entered everyone's ballots into the ballot box, the party was in full swing. Only, it was *not* going the way I'd planned. People completely understood the sock ball idea. In fact, there were so many pairs of balled-up socks being thrown around that, in some corners, you couldn't see the gym floor.

But it was also supposed to be a dance.

And *nobody* was dancing.

Mike and Hassan were trying to throw socks into the basketball nets, and a bunch of them were already stuck. Connor, Mark, Rob, and two other fifth graders I didn't know were running around trying to nail each other in the head with sock balls. A whole bunch of kids were crowding around the dumb duck, asking questions while Pou held its leash and Shady sat in a corner, obsessively scribbling on little scraps of paper like he always does. Crystal and Mary, some fifth graders from Room 12, had tied a whole bunch of socks into a long rope and were trying to skip with it.

Luckily, I had an idea for how to dial down the chaos and start the dancing.

I walked over and yelled into DJ Doozy's ear. He nodded. The hip-hop song he'd been playing faded. The strobe lights stopped revolving and were replaced by a warm, red glow, and the opening bars of "My Hero"—the most romantic song of all time—began. Connor didn't know it yet, but this was our song. The one I played over and over in my bedroom when I was thinking of him. It was his big chance to ask me to slow dance.

I caught his eye from across the gym and smiled. He gave a little wave back. Dylan nudged his shoulder. I couldn't hear from all the way across the gym, but obviously I knew the basics of what he was saying. "Ask her to dance, idiot!" or "Pearl's looking at you!" Something like that.

"Oh my God. I think he's definitely getting ready to ask you." Rebecca squeezed my arm. As one of my best friends, she knew how much I'd been dreaming of this moment.

"Do you think so?" I asked modestly, even though I knew it was true. He'd just taken a step forward. In less than a minute, we'd be dancing. Then—

"Oh my goodness, look!" Shushanna yelled.

"She's dancing." Tanya was pointing across the gym to where Shady was standing, holding his duck's leash.

"That's the cutest thing," Tamille screeched.

Illuminated by the soft red lighting, the stupid duck was swaying from side to side in perfect time to the music.

"Guys! Do the ducky!" Mark yelled. He started to sway. Then Connor and some of the other guys started doing it too. Before long, most of the kids on both sides of the gym were slow dancing alone, swaying back and forth like dumb-looking ducks...and before I could do a single thing about it, "My Hero" was fading out, and a song with a heavy bass line was taking its place.

Worst of all, the duck seemed to like that one even better.

She bopped her head from left to right and shuffled her webbed feet forward across the floor while Shady—wearing his tacky sunglasses—followed, holding the leash. Pouya was right behind him, like always.

I can't remember who joined them next to start the conga line, but I'll never forget the way it bounced and snaked around the gym for almost the entire rest of the dance—or how, after the confetti cannons were fired, the lights came up, and it was time to make the announcement of the grand-prize winner, this happened:

"And the winner is..." I said into the microphone. I

reached into the ballot box to retrieve the name of the lucky student. "Svenrietta!"

People started laughing.

I didn't get why.

"Svenrietta," I repeated. "Come get your prize." I'd never heard the name before, but I figured it was a new ESL student from a different class. Sometimes they come and go so fast it's hard to keep track of them.

"The duck won the tablet!" someone announced.

"Woo-hoo! Svenrietta!" Pouya pushed Shady forward to claim the prize. When he stepped up and took it from me with his head hung low, all the kids went wild.

At the time, I just stood there, confused.

It wasn't until later—when we were picking up the last of the socks, and I dumped the ballots into the recycling bin—that I got angry. One ballot caught my eye. *Svenrietta.* Then another. *Svenrietta.* I started unfolding them.

Svenrietta. Svenrietta. Svenrietta. Svenrietta. Svenrietta. Svenrietta. Svenrietta. Svenrietta. Svenrietta. Svenrietta. Svenrietta. Svenrietta. Svenrietta. Svenrietta.

There were no fewer than fifty ballots with her name.

Ducks don't buy socks.

There was something foul going on, and it might have had the duck's name written all over it, but I was almost certain it was Pouya Fard's doing.

The Bronson High School
FILM FANATICS CLUB

December 4
This week's assignment: Watch *Citizen Kane*

MOVIE SYNOPSIS:
In his film debut, twenty-five-year-old Orson Welles created a masterpiece in *Citizen Kane*. The story unfolds in flashbacks as a reporter researches the life of the wealthy and powerful newspaper magnate Charles Foster Kane.

WHAT PARENTS NEED TO KNOW:
Citizen Kane has some adult themes. However, it is a must-see portrait of the early twentieth century for any student who has a budding interest in film.

Made in 1941, it's thought by some to be the best movie of all time, both for its audacious techniques and for the depth of its characterization. Several scenes show characters drinking, and there is smoking throughout. Kane's affair has an impact on the plot, but there is no overt sexuality or offensive language.

CHAPTER 7

Pascale

Told by Manda

Pascale Mercier was—without a doubt—the coolest girl I'd ever laid eyes on. I mean, her name alone. Pas-cale. Passss-kall. *So French*. And not in a French teacher kind of way.

She had dark, almost black hair that she cut short and wore messy. And she always had a scarf on, even inside. Woolly ones, flowing ones, flowered ones, striped ones. Draped around her neck and thrown over one shoulder in this not-even-trying way.

Of course, I'd never considered trying to be friends with her. After my dad forced me to join the Film Fanatics club, I sat two rows back from her every Thursday after school from three thirty till four thirty. Once I stepped on the toe of her chic ankle boot when I went up to get a permission slip for the end-of-year film club social. And on the first day of school that September she'd half smiled at me in the hallway when I was trying to get to my new locker. We did that awkward thing where you both try too hard to get out of each other's way and end up dodging in the same direction. But besides that, we barely existed in the same orbit.

Needless to say, I wasn't exactly cool and collected when she actually talked to me. And not only talked to me—but somehow knew my name!

"I don't have enough copies of the DVD," said Mr. Maloney that Thursday. He was passing out *Citizen Kane* for a watch-at-home assignment. "You'll have to get together and share. And don't forget to keep thinking about your film projects for entry into the National Film Society contest. We start filming in two weeks, so I need project plans from each group by next week."

I didn't get a copy, so I glanced over at my friends Carly and Beth, who were sitting one row back and across the aisle.

Carly held up a DVD. "How about we watch it tomorrow after school at my place?" she said to me and Beth. "We can work on our plan too."

They'd settled on our film idea months ago. It was going to be called *Drop It Like It's Hot*. A modern dance-movie remake inspired by the classic rom-com *Some Like It Hot*, starring Marilyn Monroe. Not exactly my thing, but it beat being the only person in the entire club who'd be working without a partner—plus, they were counting on me to help them win, since they barely knew how to use the editing software.

"But first let's go to the Beanery," Beth added.

"Oh, Macchiato Man, flex those milk-frothing muscles!" Carly batted her eyelashes.

"Shut up!" Beth whacked Carly on the shoulder, but not hard. They were having a good day. Sometimes, I could have sworn the only reason they kept me around was to complain about each other to me when they were fighting, which was often.

Macchiato Man was a barista at the Beanery. He had a Celtic knot armband tattoo, and Beth was in love with him—despite never having talked to him except to say "medium caramel macchiato" and "thanks." Going to the Beanery in and of itself would take an hour—when you factored in sitting at the table in the corner while looking/trying not to look at the barista and guessing if he was looking/trying not to look our way—then Carly's brothers would be playing video games on the good TV. By the time we actually got around to watching the movie and talking about the project, it'd be at least five thirty. Could I take that much Carly and Beth time?

Plus, Shady and Pou were already getting babysat by Angie Murray on Thursdays—and once a week was enough. When she first started, they mostly hid from her in the basement so they could hang out with Svenrietta in the bathroom. But lately Angie had decided she wanted to go to college for early childhood education, and she was getting all ambitious about providing educational babysitting experiences.

"She made flash cards," Pouya had told me the week before. "With pictures and words…like 'car' and 'balloon.' I think she thinks we're morons."

Shady had started laughing, his whole body shaking, and Pouya joined in. "Shady! Shady! What's this?" Pouya held up a Kleenex box. "Is it a rubber boot?"

Shady nodded vigorously, sat down on the rug, and started cramming his foot into it.

"That's because you *are* morons." I grabbed the box away. And I laughed, too, but really I was thinking, *Seriously, Angie?* Now I was going to need to get my mom to talk to her about that.

"I can't," I told Carly and Beth. "I have to babysit my brother."

"Oh. Right," Beth said, but kind of snippy.

"We forgot," Carly added in a how-could-we-forget way. Lately they'd been getting more and more irritated with me, always for the same reason.

And *that* was when it happened.

"Hey. Manda. I have a copy." Pascale Mercier herself was suddenly standing by my desk. "You can watch it with me another day if that works better."

"Oh...I..." I stammered stupidly. "I mean, thanks, but no. I mean, *not* no. Just, really, thanks. But I can probably download it or something." Almost immediately, I felt like kicking myself. *Why did I need to jump straight to being my maximum socially awkward self and mess up my one chance to actually get to know her?* Thankfully, Pascale gave me another shot.

"You'd probably have to pay to download it. Why bother?

I've got it right here." She waved the copy Mr. Maloney had loaned her. "We'll watch it at your place if you have to babysit."

Which was how—on the afternoon of Monday, December 8—Pascale Mercier, her scarf, and I ended up walking together to my house, stopping along the way to pick up Shady, Pouya, and Svenrietta. I'd begged Mom to just let them walk home alone, but despite lots of community outrage, the police still hadn't managed to catch the Banana Bandit. In fact, it was getting worse. He'd struck twice that week, and even though his targets were always old ladies, my mom said no way. It was too dangerous.

"Sorry," I said to Pascale as we stood in the schoolyard. "They should be out any minute."

I glanced around. There were baggy-eyed moms in puffy parkas, and take-out coffee cups littered the ground around the garbage can. A little kid who was standing beside us was whacking the fence with a stick, like smashing it to shreds was his only goal in life. I willed him with every fiber of my being to please stop before he annoyed Pascale.

I tried to catch her eye to share a look like *Oh my God. This place, huh?* but she had her scarf pulled up over her face, probably trying to filter out the sounds and stench of elementary school. Finally, the bell rang, and the doors opened. Kids poured out, but it was another few minutes before Shady and Pouya emerged.

Shady had Svenrietta in her sling, tucked under his coat, so all you could see was her head poking out. And it's saying something that the fact my brother was carrying a duck wasn't the thing that made Pascale do a double take.

"*What* is on your head?" I asked Pouya.

My brother's friend grinned. "You mean, *what* is on my top branch. Behold! I am the Christmas tree!"

"Okay." I didn't want an explanation—especially not in front of Pascale—but Pouya launched into one anyway.

"You know I've been pretty bummed out lately, right? With the end of the world coming? But then I realized I'd been looking at it all wrong," Pou went on. "I mean, the world is ending. That's a fact."

Pascale raised her eyebrows, and I gave Pouya a withering, please-shut-up look.

"It is!" he insisted. "In case you live under a rock, the fourth sign came to pass yesterday. *Great winged machines will fall from the sky!*"

"Okay, *what* are you talking about?" I said with an embarrassed laugh. "I didn't see any falling machines."

"The planes!" Pouya gestured wildly with his hands. "In Austin, Texas, and London, England. Don't you read the papers?"

"Oh. That," I said.

"Oh that?" Pouya echoed. "Seven hundred and twenty-one people died, Manda!"

I glanced sideways at Pascale to see if she thought I was a jerk. I hadn't meant it that way. Just that, yes, the plane crashes that had randomly happened in two separate places the day before were horrible, but they weren't a sign of the end of the world.

"Anyway," Pouya went on. "I realized...when the world is ending, you've got two choices. You can either mope around and dread it, or you can live every moment to the max."

He pointed to the headband he was wearing—which had a giant sparkling star on a spring. "So I tried out for the Christmas play. I beat five other people for the lead role." He hopped forward, holding his arms out from his sides in an upside-down V. The star bobbled as he jumped.

Pascale looked puzzled—or maybe amused? It was hard to tell.

"So? You're hopping around like a weirdo?" I asked.

"I'm getting in character," Pou explained. "The play is less than two weeks away! And obviously trees can't walk."

I didn't bother pointing out that trees can't hop either, or talk, or that being the tree sounded like probably the worst role in the whole play—more pointless than being one of eight reindeer, even. I just wanted to get home, so Pascale and I could get far away from Pouya and Shady.

"Guys, this is Pascale," I said as I started walking.

"Hi." Pascale gave a little wave with her brown leather glove—so much cooler than my puffy, waterproof Gore-Tex mitts.

Shady didn't answer, of course, and thankfully Pouya was too busy being a tree to make much conversation. As the rest of us walked, he hopped along behind.

As soon as we got home, I went straight into damage control.

"You guys can play unlimited video games if you leave us alone. But first put Svenrietta in the basement."

I motioned for Pascale to follow me into the kitchen.

"Do you like brie?" I said casually. I already had our snack prepared: a plate of fancy cheeses, sliced pear, and crackers—but not Ritz. Nice ones with little pieces of oats in them. Pascale smiled and shrugged, which I took as a yes, but before I could get the cheese, my brother came in, took his sunglasses off, and glared at me as he lifted Svenrietta out of her sling and set her down on the floor.

She immediately started quacking—loudly—and preening herself, which is what she always does when she comes out of the sling. Feathers were flying everywhere as she shook her wings and nibbled at her chest with her beak.

"Shady!" I yelled over the quacking. "I said basement." But I could tell from the look on his face that he wasn't giving in. Svenrietta was still sleeping in the basement bathroom because of Mom's rules, and she always had to stay down there when our parents had company. But sometimes after dinner, Mom and Dad let Shady bring her upstairs, and after school I usually let her wander around the house until about five minutes before Mom got home. Shady knew the regular after-school routine, and my brother was nothing if not set in his ways.

Pouya hopped into the kitchen and over to the fridge to

get a pack of frozen peas. Again, aside from the hopping, this
was normal after-school stuff, but this *wasn't* a normal day.

"Svenri!" he called. The duck stopped preening and stood
at full attention. Pouya tossed a pea in the air, and she caught
it in her beak and gobbled it. He threw another and another.

I took the plastic wrap off the snack plate as quickly as I
could. "Sorry," I said to Pascale. "My house is kind of weird.
We can go watch the movie in my room if you want."

But she was focused on the duck, who was flapping back
and forth catching peas. So mortifying! Only…

"Can I try?" she asked. It was the longest sentence she'd
said since we'd met on the front steps after school.

My brother nodded.

"It's better if you throw them high," Pouya explained,
passing over the peas. "It gives her more time to catch them."

Pascale threw a few and laughed out loud—a sound like
little bells—each time Svenri caught one.

"What else can she do?" Pascale asked.

Shady showed her.

Sit. Stand. Come here. Quack! And of course, her best trick
of all. Shady grabbed my phone and turned on some music.
Pascale clapped her hands in delight when the duck danced.

"I adore her!" she cried.

Meanwhile, Pouya had hopped over to the fridge and started piling a plate with snacks. I watched in dismay as Pascale picked a packet of string cheese off the top when we walked past.

"Brie tastes a bit like feet to me," she said apologetically. "Slimy feet."

I'd tried a piece the night before. She wasn't entirely wrong.

"I like these though." She took some fancy crackers off the plate I'd prepared. Then we went upstairs to watch the movie, but barely ten minutes in—at the part when Thompson gets assigned to investigate Kane's death—she hit Pause.

"I have a thought," she said.

I was expecting her to say something insightful about the cinematography, but instead she grinned. "For our film project," she explained. "I mean, if you want to be my partner."

My heart skipped a beat. Beth and Carly were going to kill me if I backed out on making their dance movie rom-com. It'd be like the time I told them I was sick when really I didn't feel like hanging out with them, then ran into them an hour later at the ice-cream place at the mall with my family. They didn't talk to me for weeks. Only, this time, it would be way worse, because I couldn't just say that my parents forced me. Beth and Carly were going to be pissed that I chose someone I barely knew over them. Plus, if I dropped out of their group and they didn't win the film contest, they'd find a way to blame me. But for a chance to be partners with Pascale Mercier? Was it worth the risk? I was really tempted to find out.

"I'm thinking of a day-in-the-life thing. And we can film it in black and white for added drama."

"Like, a documentary?" I asked.

"Yes! Exactly!"

"But a day in the life of who?"

"A domesticated duck, of course!" she said, like it was obvious. "It's so unique and interesting."

I didn't know about *that*. Svenrietta mostly ate, quacked, and made a huge mess wherever she went.

All the same, I found myself grinning like an idiot.

"Yeah. That could work," I said. "A duck documentary."

"A duckumentary!" Pascale said, with her little bells of laughter.

"A duckumentary." I nodded. "Okay. I'm excited." And I really was—even if it was in an *oh my God, what am I doing, I might puke* kind of way. But as sick as I felt about blowing up my entire social life (as sad as that social life was to begin with), if I was being honest with myself, I was already all-in. Chances like this one didn't come along every day, especially not for someone like me. I was going to get to be actual film-project partners (and possibly even friends) with Pascale Mercier!

Duck Tales in the Library at Recess!

Svenrietta loves stories! Sign up here for a fifteen-minute
time slot to read to her in the library.

MONDAY	TUESDAY	WEDNESDAY	THURSDAY	FRIDAY
11:00–11:15	11:00–11:15	11:00–11:15	11:00–11:15	11:00–11:15
Aisha	Mark	Margot	Tamille	Carly
11:15–11:30	11:15–11:30	11:15–11:30	11:15–11:30	11:15–11:30
Shiori	Amber	Jasmine	Hassan	Spencer R.
11:30–11:45	11:30–11:45	11:30–11:45	11:30–11:45	11:30–11:45
Ida	Naomi	Arjana	Linn	Michaela

If you can't make it, remember to let Mrs. Patton know so we can give
your spot to another student. We want to make sure everyone gets a
turn. Also, please come five minutes early to choose the book you
want to read, and remember to use your indoor voice and to put your
book in the returns bin when you're finished with it.

CHAPTER 8

Duck Tales

Told by Pouya

The read-to-a-duck club was Shady's psychiatrist's idea. I heard his mom talking on the phone about it. It was supposed to trick Shady into talking, somehow. That was never going to work, but it gave us something to do at recess—which meant we didn't have to go out in the cold—and an activity to do now that we'd dropped out of Environment Club. (Because, really, what's the point of saving an environment that's going to explode in twenty days?) Plus, Svenrietta had great taste in books.

The scary ones about true-life events were her favorites: haunted hotels, abandoned schools where you could still

hear the footsteps of old students, waterfalls where someone had died tragically and now hikers see their ghostly
reflection. You could tell she was listening to every word.

Sometimes, when kids were reading, Svenrietta sat on
Shady's lap. Sometimes she sat with me. Sometimes she sat with
the kid who was reading, and other times—especially when
the book was boring—she wandered around getting feathers
all over the carpet. Today was a wandering day. Tamille had
picked a book about sea otters, and Svenri just wasn't into it.

"Adult sea otters type-eye-sally..." Tamille squinted at
the page. "Type-ee-sally," she tried again. "Type-e-kally. Oh,
typically." Svenrietta, who had been busy pecking at Shady's
shoelace, glanced up approvingly. "Typically we-eye-gh..."
Tamille pressed on.

"Weigh!" Pearl Summers was suddenly standing over us
with an armload of books. "It says *weigh*. And can you guys
please move? I need to shelve these."

Like I said, the best part was getting to stay indoors
for recess, but I haven't mentioned the worst part: Pearl
Summers. She and her friends Rebecca and Monica help
Mrs. Patton reshelve books at recess, and ever since the
Sock Ball, when Svenrietta won the tablet, Pearl totally had

it out for me—even though I'd had nothing to do with it.

I had a good guess who did though. Every time I asked him if he wrote those ballots, Shady just smiled into his chest and shrugged, but when he showed up at school with a note from his mom saying that Svenrietta wanted to donate the tablet to the library so kids could sign it out and everyone could share it, I knew for sure.

"Move!" Pearl said again.

Tamille shifted over obediently, and so did Shady, but I stood my ground.

"This is the Duck Tales area." I motioned to the space around us. "We're doing important work here." Svenrietta ruffled her feathers as if agreeing. "You'll have to come back later."

Pearl glared at me. "Well, the *Duck Tales area*"—she said that part like it was some kind of toxic waste dump— "happens to be right in front of Graphic Novels A–J, and that was there first. So, move! Before I go and tell Mrs. Patton this duck is being disruptive again."

I would have ignored Pearl. I mean, let her try! Other than the fact that Svenri was nibbling Shady's shoelace, she wasn't bothering anyone.

But Shady tugged at my sleeve, telling me to shift over. He had a point. Svenrietta was still officially "on probation" when it came to being allowed at school.

Mrs. Mackie said Svenri had already been disruptive once—and, okay, she *had* caused chaos when she got freaked out by the janitor's mop, broke off her leash, and ran into a kindergarten classroom quacking like a maniac and making a bunch of kids cry.

It meant Svenrietta only had two strikes left in Mrs. Mackie's "three strikes and you're out" system. I could understand why Shady didn't want to risk it.

I bum scooched forward to let Pearl in behind me, but I made sure to stick my tongue out at her while I was doing it.

"Oh my God!" Pearl exclaimed before Tamille could get back to reading about sea otters. She wasn't talking to us. Just talking loudly! In the library! In case you want an example of being disruptive!

"The new Champions Club book is in." She held it up to show Rebecca, who was shelving on the other side of the library.

Tamille looked up from her sea-otter book with wide eyes. "I want to read that so much," she said. "I love horses."

"Yeah, well. Sorry." Pearl hugged it to her chest. "I'm checking it out today. Then Rebecca probably wants it."

"Definitely," Rebecca said. "I've got second dibs."

"That's not fair," I pointed out. "Just because you shelve books?"

"It's one of the perks." Pearl shrugged. "Anyway, Tamille can barely get through a baby book." She wrinkled her nose in the direction of *Learning to Read, Series 1: Sea Otters!* "She wouldn't understand Champions Club number seven. No offense, Tamille," Pearl added.

That was when I saw Shady's feet tensing up inside his sneakers. Feet aren't something most people notice, but it's something I've gotten good at, being Shady's friend. When he's nervous or upset and he's sitting, his toes *tap-tap-tap* at the air. If he's standing, his heels grind into the ground like they're trying to dig a hole. Happy feet bounce. And mad feet are tight with the toes pointed forward or tilted back. I'd seen his feet a lot of ways, but never quite so angry before.

"I can read anything I want in Croatian. Anyway, I like looking at the pictures," Tamille answered in a small voice. "And I can read English. Just not the really hard words yet."

While Tamille was talking, Shady slowly reached into his pocket. I wouldn't have noticed it except that Svenrietta snapped to attention. Ducks have excellent sideways vision because their eyes are on the sides of their heads. They also have good hearing—especially for food noises.

"I'm not saying you can't borrow it." Pearl was lecturing Tamille. "I'm just saying you have to wait your turn. It's because—" But before she could say why she deserved the book more, Shady tossed a handful of cracked corn near her feet.

Svenrietta started quacking. She flapped her wings frantically, trying to get the food, and her body lifted off the ground, but only a little. She isn't much of a flyer.

"Oh my God! Get it away!" Pearl shrieked. She started kicking, but that only made Svenrietta more flustered and flappy. She does *not* like people getting in the way of her cracked corn. Then Pearl went and made it even worse by dropping her pile of books. One of them landed right on Svenrietta's back. Thankfully, it was a paperback, but it still freaked her out pretty badly.

WAK! WAK! WAK!

Mrs. Patton came running over, and Pearl didn't waste a second before going into tattletale mode.

"Mrs. Patton!" she wailed over the quacking. "Shady threw duck food near me, and then his duck started going crazy. We need to report this to Mrs. Mackie."

Shady picked up Svenrietta. The second he had her in his arms, she settled right down.

"Shady, is that true?" Mrs. Patton asked.

Shady had been doing pretty great with yes and no answers lately, but now he went right back to the way he was before and couldn't answer. I could tell from the way he looked down at the floor and how his shoulders tightened up that he was upset. Even just the idea of getting in trouble at school upsets Shady.

"Shady would never bring food into the library," I said. At least, he'd never bring *people* food into the library.

I pointed to the floor, where the evidence was clearly in our favor. There wasn't a single piece of cracked corn on the carpet (ducks are food vacuums), but there were graphic novels all over the place.

"She was quacking because Pearl dropped a book on her," I said.

"Pearl," Mrs. Patton said. "That could have hurt the duck. Try to be more careful, okay?" Mrs. Patton bent down and started picking up books. She placed them in a stack on the table for Pearl to finish shelving—which Pearl did, with a murderous look in her eye, shoving them in any which way.

Tamille went back to reading aloud to Svenrietta, but she'd only made it through another page or so when the bell rang.

"Hey!" Pearl shouted. She was down to just two books left to shelve. She held them both up. One had fairies on the front, and the other seemed to be about space. "Where's Champions Club number seven?"

Nobody answered.

"It was here a minute ago. Who stole it?"

"Don't look at me," I said.

"Tamille!" Pearl accused. But Tamille held up her empty hands. She didn't have a backpack with her either. Unless she ate it, she didn't have the book.

"You probably put it on the shelf by accident," I said.

Shady handed me the leash that he kept in Svenri's diaper bag, and I reattached it to her harness while he went to put the sea-otter book in the returns bin.

"You want me to help you get to the sensory room?" I asked when he came back.

We were going to be playing jai alai in gym class that day. It's a game where you bounce a ball against the wall with a scoop thing. Svenrietta hates the echoey noises of the balls slamming against the walls, and Shady can't handle it either—so they were going to do a yoga video in the special needs room instead. But wherever Svenri went, Shady had to take all her stuff. Not just the diaper bag, but also her food and water.

Shady nodded, so we both headed to the sensory room with me carrying the food bag.

"All good?" I asked, once we'd set everything down on the foam mats beside the beanbag chairs. It was all stuff that Jackson Eriks's grandparents fundraised for with an autism-awareness walk last year.

Shady nodded before plopping down into the hammock swing in the corner with Svenri in his lap. He twirled his feet lazily to twist the swing up in a knot. That was when I saw that he was grinning big-time.

"What?" I asked.

He lifted his feet and let the swing start to spin in circles, and as it twirled, he laughed...out loud. It was the funniest sound. Not because he laughed funny or anything—it wasn't especially low or high or donkey-like. It was your average *ha-ha-ha*. I'd just never heard him do it before, so it sounded weird.

"What is it?" I couldn't help it. I started laughing, too, even though I didn't know what we were laughing about yet.

Shady stopped the swing with his feet, then leaned down, still smiling wide. He reached into Svenri's diaper bag and pulled something out.

Champions Club #7.

"You stole it?"

Shady shook his head vigorously. He took out the due-date slip and pointed to his name on it. Fair point. You can't steal a library book. They're for everyone.

"Well, why'd you take it out? You don't seriously want to read that, do you?"

I don't have anything against horses, but Champions Club books are all about girls who are obsessed with gossiping about each other and winning trophies.

Shady stuck out his tongue like *bleh* so I knew he felt the same way. Then he bit his lip, seeming frustrated. There was more he wanted to tell me, but he couldn't. He looked around the room, then held up one finger, like *wait*. I watched while he rooted through a bin of school supplies on the table and pulled out a pad of sticky notes. He handed me Svenri, who was getting heavy enough that it took two arms to hold her, then walked over to a big laminated poster on the wall. He started to sticky it up—which took a while—but, thankfully, the teacher supervisor who was supposed to watch him was running late.

STRATEGIES FOR TAKING CHARGE OF MY FEELINGS AND BEHAVIORS

- Make a fist and squeeze hard.
- Think about a safe place.
- Count slowly for 20 breaths.
- Squeeze or press down on something.
- Give the teacher my "I need a break" card.
- Draw a picture and write your feelings underneath.

This integrated education resource is brought to you by K.Y. Autism Awareness.

I stared at it, amazed. *Taking charge of makin' a safe place for the underducks.* Not only was it cool that he'd found the words he needed in the poster, but I was pretty sure I understood now, and I liked the idea.

"You're going to give the book to Tamille, right?"

He nodded.

"Because underducks are like underdogs!" I went on.

I'd learned that word not long ago. It meant someone who was never going to win because the odds were against them. Like Tamille, because she has to catch up to fifth-grade reading level in a whole other language, or me and Aisha, because our families can't afford to buy forty pairs of socks for homeless people.

Actually, now that I thought of it, there were lots of underducks at Carleton Elementary—from the kids who lived in the big, rent-controlled apartment buildings in Summerside, like my family and Aisha's; to the special-ed kids, like Shady because of his not-talking thing and Jackson Eriks and Aaron Somers-Thanning, who have autism; to boys like DuShawn Henry, who gets teased because he wears his hair long and likes dresses; to the ones who've just moved here from another place and don't know the rules yet; to the ones whose families are a little different because they've got grandparents instead of parents, or two moms, or no mom at all—and we were all overdue for some better odds.

Taking charge of making a safe place for the underducks. Not only did it sound kind of fun—it was exactly the kind of mission that was worthy of our last three weeks on Earth.

"Killer move, Captain!" I held up my hand for a high five. Shady didn't leave me hanging. Then he passed me the book hopefully.

"I'll get it to Tamille," I promised.

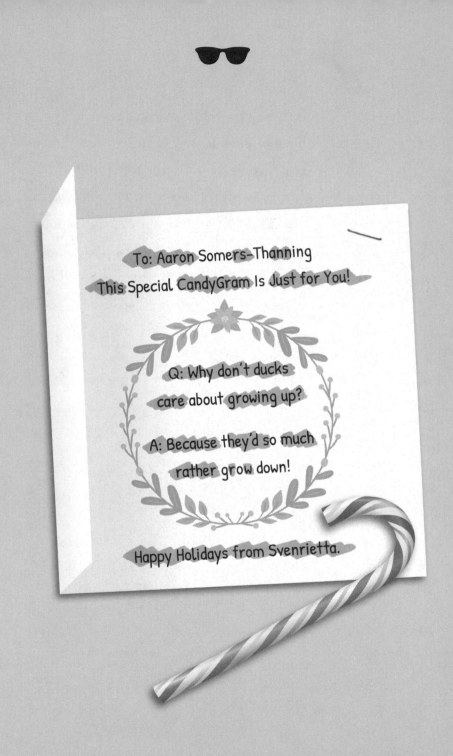

To: Aaron Somers-Thanning

This Special CandyGram Is Just for You!

Q: Why don't ducks care about growing up?

A: Because they'd so much rather grow down!

Happy Holidays from Svenrietta.

CHAPTER 9

The Underducks

Told by Manda

When Pascale and I ran the idea for our duckumentary past Mr. Maloney at Film Fanatics club, he was completely on board. He even called Mrs. Mackie, the principal at Shady's school, to ask if she'd grant us access to film there, and he got us time off from class to do it. We had two days and a lot of footage to gather, so we tried not to waste time setting up that first morning. Easier said than done though. The kids were all over us.

"Can I be in your movie?" a girl with red braids asked. "I acted once in a commercial for a shoe store."

"What's this button do?" Pascale had to swat away the

hand of an overeager second grader who couldn't take his eyes off the camera.

"Are you from Hollywood?" a wide-eyed, gap-toothed kindergartner asked.

"Okay, Zach. Come put your backpack away." His teacher guided him toward the coat hooks, but the whole time he was watching us over his shoulder with his mouth hanging open.

"Let's get a few establishing shots," I suggested as the hallway emptied out. "Maybe some of these little snow boots and a few turkey crafts." I pointed to a bulletin board that hadn't been updated since Thanksgiving. "Stuff that screams 'elementary school.'"

"Good idea." Pascale loosened her scarf like she was ready to get down to business.

She held the portable LED light as I panned the hand-held, high-definition camera slowly down the hallway. It was undeniable: we made a great team. Right from the concept, "a day in the life of a service duck," to the execution, "strictly observational with narration, no interviews," to the style, "dramatic but with a goofy, educational edge—like film noir meets *Sesame Street*," we saw eye to eye.

It also helped that, right from the start, Shady was comfortable around Pascale. She never teased him or made a thing of it when he didn't answer her questions or only answered them in his own way. The star of the show thought Pascale was pretty awesome too. Although that might have been because she started carrying a bag of peas in her pocket.

"Just keep panning until you get to the classroom door." Pascale walked a few steps ahead while staying just out of the shot. She peered in the door of Room 9. "Then you can come in tight for a shot of Svenri sitting on Shady's desk wearing...a tiny elf hat? For some reason?" Pascale said those last two parts like questions, but not in a weirded-out way. She seemed to take everything in stride—no matter what kind of odd things Shady and Pouya did—and they were definitely doing something odd that day. In fact, I might not have believed it if I hadn't seen it with my own eyes and filmed it with my own camera.

I got the shot, then handed the camera to Pascale so she could review the footage on the display.

"Oh," I said as I watched Mrs. Okah pick up a wrapper a kid had dropped on the carpet. "Svenri's wearing the elf hat because it's CandyGrams day."

It had been almost five years since I'd been a student at Carleton Elementary. You'd think I would have overcome the trauma, but the sight of Pearl Summers and a bunch of other high-ponytailed popular girls walking up and down the aisles with big stockings full of little folded cards (each with a small candy cane stapled inside) still gave me the shivers.

"What's CandyGrams?" Pascale asked with her eyes still on the camera display.

"It's basically a Christmas popularity contest," I explained. "Friends buy little candy canes for each other for twenty-five cents each. Then when they get delivered the next day, all the loners get to feel like nobodies because they don't get any."

I'd been there, done that. Especially after my best friend, Meghan, moved away halfway through fifth grade. Only— something was different this year. All the CandyGrams had been passed out, and Mrs. Okah was already partway into a lesson about words with silent letters before I figured out what it was: every single kid in the room was either sucking on a mini candy cane or had one on their desk. Some of them were different though. They looked like the cherry-flavored ones (the good kind), and nobody seemed to be on the verge of tears.

Then, as we were packing up our equipment to follow Svenrietta and the rest of the class to the music room, I overheard a boy named Jackson, who was sucking on a cherry candy cane, ask a girl named Aisha: "What's your card say?"

"'What do you call a duck that steals?'" she read slowly and carefully from her CandyGram.

"What?" he asked.

"'A robber duck.'" She smiled, then read the rest. "'Happy holidays from Svenrietta.' How about yours?"

"'What do you see when a duck bends over?'" He was already grinning from ear to ear. "Its butt quack."

I heard a familiar burst of laughter from across the room. So familiar that it made my breath catch in my throat. It couldn't be. But when I looked up, it definitely was...

Shady was sitting at his desk, doubled over—snort-laughing like the time our dad walked into the screen door with a plate of hamburgers. Meanwhile, Pouya was yukking it up beside him.

"What?" Pouya said when he caught me staring. "It's funny!"

Shady managed to catch his breath, only to crack up again.

Was this honestly the same kid who'd been too anxious to even smile when class photos had been taken a few months before?

After music—where Svenrietta joined in by pecking at the triangle Shady was playing—the bell rang for recess, and things got weirder. Most of the kids rushed out, but Pascale and I stayed behind with Shady and Pouya to get shots of my brother putting on Svenrietta's duck boots (another thing my mom read about on a message board and ordered online, since now, besides selective mutism message boards, she was also a lurker on duck-care forums). After that, Shady had to get Svenri settled into her sling. By the time we got out, recess was almost half over.

"It's so pretty," Pascale remarked.

It really was. The snow was coming down in big, fat flakes and had already completely covered the cracked concrete of the playground. Seen from a distance, anyway, there was something sweet and innocent about the scene— all those kids in their bright scarves and hats, laughing and running around. But it only took a second for the illusion to shatter.

One big kid in a gray coat and another wearing an orange hat came charging across the yard toward a snowman that a couple of little kids were building.

"Hiiiyah!" Gray Coat kicked the snowman in the head, then Orange Hat finished it off with a mitten-clad karate chop.

"Seriously, guys?!" Pascale yelled at them.

I shook my head, but I wasn't surprised. Grade school hadn't changed much after all.

That was when I felt Shady push past me. He marched straight toward the snowman.

"Yup. That's what I was thinking too," Pouya said as he followed. "Those kids are definite underducks."

"Definite whats?" I asked, but Pouya was too far ahead to answer. Pascale and I had to run to catch up.

When we reached the snowman, one of the little girls was sitting on the ground with tears in her eyes. "Teacher!" she said plaintively to me. "They broke Mr. Snowy."

"I'm not a teacher," I said, but I was kind of flattered. Most people tell me I look young for my age.

"It's okay." Pouya offered a hand to help her up. "Look!" He packed some snow into his mitten. "It's perfect snowman snow today. We'll rebuild him. Even better than before. Right, Shady?"

My brother nodded, then took Svenri out of her sling and showed the girl how to gently stroke the duck's head. She pulled off her mitten, and as she petted Svenri, she blinked her tears away. Her friend came over to see too.

It was amazing footage of a service duck in action, and Pascale and I got every second of it.

Meanwhile, Pouya was working in the background with a little boy to pat the snowman's head back together. They were just finishing up when the big kid with the orange hat walked past. "Want to film us smashing it again?" he asked.

"Get lost!" I shouted, and I automatically stepped in front of my brother.

But Shady walked around me and stood in front. Then he set Svenrietta down in the snow and crossed his arms defiantly.

"Good idea," Pouya said, coming to stand beside him. "We'll guard it with our lives. Go pick on a snowperson your own size!" he shouted to the big kids.

Shady clapped twice, telling Svenrietta to stay close, then

he began to lead her in a big circle around the snowman on her leash. Once the kids were a safe distance away, Pouya joined the march, defending the perimeter.

The kid with the gray coat pointed and laughed, but he didn't come any closer, and when the class went out later to do a science unit on snowflakes as part of the water cycle, Mr. Snowy was still standing.

Then—and this was maybe the biggest deal of all—Shady raised his hand and pointed toward the hallway to ask to use the bathroom during final-period gym class. It meant we didn't have to rush home right after school. Instead we took the long way, wandering down the main street through Summerside, filming as we went.

A family on their way home from school stopped to fuss over Svenrietta. Next, she sat for a while with a homeless man on the corner of Bloor and Sunnydale, letting him stroke her feathers. He told Shady and Pouya how he used to raise ducks and chickens on a farm when he was a kid. The memory made him smile widely, showing a broken front tooth. "You're a good girl, aren't ya?" he said to Svenri.

We went into a café and bought him a doughnut, and he

clapped his hands when Svenri came toward him, carrying the bag in her bill. "Now that's service!"

It was a good day. A *really* good day. One of the best I'd seen Shady have in, well, ages. Maybe ever.

Which made what happened next all the worse.

7 Tips for Surviving the End of the World

Brought to You by the Apocalypse Preparedness Squad

1. Don't panic!

2. Look for others who are friendly and want to live together. It's way easier to survive in a group than alone.

3. Put together a survival kit. Some things you might want to include are bottled water, bandages, a flashlight, warm socks, rope, duct tape, and matches for starting a fire (but make sure they're the waterproof kind).

4. If you come face-to-face with a wild animal, your first response might be to run away screaming, but that can trigger the animal's predatory instinct. Sometimes hiding and staying quiet is the best idea.

5. Stay warm and dry. Carry fresh socks, and wear layers and a hat to conserve your body heat.

6. Look for sources of clean water and stay hydrated.

7. And remember, DON'T PANIC!!!

CHAPTER 10

Stealing the Show

Told by Pearl Summers

Elfina is the most important role in *Santa's Tree Trouble*, this year's holiday musical. Without her, Santa (played by Connor) would never realize the havoc being caused by Elves 1, 2, and 3 or learn to see the true beauty in the scraggly old pine tree (unfortunately, played by Pouya). Christmas would basically be ruined.

Also, Elfina has a solo *and* the most lines. It wasn't surprising that Mrs. Carlisle chose me for the part. People say I have a beautiful singing voice and a natural stage presence.

Unfortunately, nobody was appreciating it that day at

rehearsal. At first, it was all the duck's fault, then it was all Pouya's.

"Okay, let's take scene one from the top," Mrs. Carlisle said. "I need Santa, the elves, and the tree."

I was already in my spot—at center stage. Elf 1, played by Rebecca, was sitting on the edge of the stage reviewing her lines, but everyone else was at the back of the gym watching the stupid duck who—I'm not even kidding—had her own film crew.

Shady's sister, Manda, and her friend Pascale—an angry-looking girl wearing a huge, flowery scarf—were on their second day of filming some kind of movie. Mrs. Mackie said we were supposed to ignore them and carry on like usual, but kids were following them everywhere like they were big-shot producers or something.

I watched in disgust as the duck waddled across a big piece of butcher paper that Shady, Arjana, and Aisha were supposed to be painting to look like the outside of Santa's workshop. If there were feathers stuck to the backdrop, I was definitely going to complain. Because this was just one more example in a long list of ways that Shady's duck had been causing trouble since she'd started coming to school—

and it was getting worse and worse.

For example, the Friday before, which was CandyGrams day, student council delivered the mini candy canes people bought for their friends only to find that there were already cherry candy canes on some kids' desks. It was mostly the kids who never participate in things—like Aisha, Tamille, DuShawn, Tammy, and Jackson. And all the candy canes had tags on them that said they were from Svenrietta. Hello! CandyGrams are supposed to be a fundraiser for the food bank! And a sign of friendship! When a duck starts giving them out for free, for no reason, the whole thing falls apart.

Then, in gym class, a few of us said we didn't want DuShawn on our relay team. (He was wearing his dress that day, and—I'm not being prejudiced—it slows him down.) And when we got back to the changing rooms, we found something gross and brown on the soles of our regular in-door shoes. Was it duck poop? I mean, I wasn't going to touch it or smell it to find out, but probably.

Finally, just that morning, after Monica and I pointed out that Aisha's hat came from Walmart and was probably produced by slave labor, we came out of class for recess to find our one hundred percent locally made Truly Northern hats missing! They turned up later in the lost and found, but by then they smelled like hot dogs and sweat. There was a feather stuck to Monica's, so I'm positive they were stolen by Pou and the duck and that even Shady was in on it! So much for any loyalty we'd built back in our sandbox days.

I took my hat straight to the office and reported the incident to Mrs. Mackie, but she just said it looked like down from someone's jacket and that we should keep our hats in our coat sleeves if we didn't want to lose them.

"I said I need the elves, Santa, and the tree, please!" Mrs. Carlisle called again when nobody had moved.

"Connor!" I called. "Hurry up!"

After all, as much as Elfina was the most important role in the play, Santa was indispensable too. Connor hadn't said that he liked me *yet*—not in so many words—but acting side by side had deepened our relationship. Just the other day, he'd held the door open for me on the way in from recess *and* asked what my favorite kind of chocolate was. *Why?* There could only be one reason. He was planning to get me a gift!

"Okay, let's take five," Shady's sister said. She'd been lying on the floor to get a duck-level shot, and when she stood up, it finally seemed to break everyone's trance. Connor, Wendel, and Monica started toward the stage.

"It's impossible to get good footage with the light changing like this, anyway," I heard Manda's friend complain. She tossed her scarf over her shoulder and looked in the direction of Mr. Nelson, the school custodian.

He was carrying cartloads of chairs through the back doors of the gym and stacking them along one wall. There were hundreds already. The gym was going to be packed on performance day, which meant we *needed* to get serious about rehearsing.

Still, Pouya had to be reminded to take his place one more time.

"Sorry," he said, leaving the group of kids he'd been standing with and jogging up to the stage. "We were just going over some APS post-Q survival tips."

Pou's Planet-Q-is-going-to-smash-into-the-world thing was beyond stupid, and the worst part was, more and more people seemed to be believing him. After he'd insisted that Gavin's black cat having a litter of ten pure-white kittens was some kind of sign, pretty much everyone but me, Rebecca, and Monica had dropped out of Friends of the

Environment Club, and a bunch of them had joined his ridiculous Apocalypse Preparedness Squad (APS) instead.

"If you're going to be like that…" Pou said, catching the you're-such-an-idiot look I was giving him, "don't come running to me asking for bottled water and canned peaches when disaster strikes."

As he talked, he put on his ridiculous bobbly-star headband, which he'd basically been wearing since he got the role of tree—even though he wasn't supposed to be decorated until the last scene. Finally, he walked to the back of the stage and spread his branches.

Mrs. Carlisle cued us.

I took a deep breath, trying to forget my frustration with Pouya and become Elfina—body and soul. "You guys!" I said loud and clear, with a smile that could blind the sun. "It's almost the most magical time of the year again!"

"You mean reindeer games playoff time?" Wendel said, overacting with a cheesy wink.

"No, silly! Christmastime!" I answered.

"Hooray!" the other elves cheered in unison—or, it was supposed to be in unison, but it was all over the place, and Elf 3 didn't sound very cheerful.

"But before we can celebrate"—I paused, held up my hands like two tabletops, and looked left and right—"we need to find the perfect gift for Santa."

I had to elbow Tanya to get her attention. "Oh. Um…" She looked for the line in her script. "I bet Santa would like a *cool* smartphone. So he can text with the snowmen."

Mrs. Carlisle interrupted. "Elves, when you give your gift idea, remember to pretend to hold up a box. Pearl, you're going to wrap those and have them ready for the next rehearsal, right?"

I nodded.

"Okay, Pouya," Mrs. Carlisle went on. "Your line now."

Pouya bumped into my shoulder and nearly knocked Wendel over as he hopped to center stage. "Yo, elves!" he said. "I bet Santa would dig getting a tree as a present."

"*Cut!*" I yelled, so loudly that even the kids painting sets at the back of the gym turned to look. "First, trees don't hop. You're planted," I said. "Second, it doesn't say 'Yo' anywhere in the script. Trees don't say 'yo'!"

"Trees don't even talk," Pouya shot back. "So, if the tree can talk, why can't it hop? I'm just giving my character some character."

"Well, don't!" I answered.

Mrs. Carlisle sighed. "Okay, guys. Pouya, no 'yo.' Pearl, I'm the one who yells 'cut,' not you. Let's try it from the top."

So, we did, but Pouya wouldn't quit hopping around and using dumb accents, and Wendel started laughing so hard he couldn't say his lines. Then when he finally did manage to say, "I think Santa might want a big flat-screen TV," he messed it up and said, "big, fat-screen TV," which made Pouya start laughing. Then Pouya got even dumber and started yodeling his lines because he wanted to be a yodeling tree.

There were only a few minutes of rehearsal left, and I'd just stepped forward for my solo when Shady's sister, Manda, started freaking out.

"Where's Svenrietta?" she yelled. "Shady? Do you have her? She was here a minute ago."

I sighed loudly.

Shady stood up, looking left and right.

"Check in the equipment closet!" Tamille suggested.

"And under the stage," someone else chimed in.

"Can we start the music now?" I asked Mrs. Carlisle. I'd been practicing "Santa Wants a Christmas Tree" every spare minute to make sure my voice would be clear as bells, and I was dying to hear how it would echo in the gym. Not to mention that Connor wouldn't be able to help falling in love with me when he heard my voice. It's been described as "angelic" on more than one occasion, and not just by my mom.

"Just a second, Pearl." Mrs. Carlisle turned away. "Mr. Nelson," she called across the gym as the janitor came in with another cartload of chairs. "Can we keep the doors closed for a few minutes, please? We have a duck on the loose."

That was when Manda's scarfy friend caused the real panic.

"What if she already got out?" She ran for the doors and pushed them open. Shady, Pouya, and a bunch of other kids dashed out into the snow with indoor shoes and no coats or hats.

Mrs. Carlisle had to run after them to tell them to come back in—and by the time they did, the bell had rung, ending rehearsal.

I sighed. Then I stormed off the stage and back to class. Honestly, I didn't care if the duck was gone forever. I hoped it was.

LOST DUCK

Please help us find Svenrietta!

Our female domesticated duck has gone missing in the area around Carleton Elementary School. She is approximately six months old and was last seen wearing a red harness and a duck diaper with blue and white hearts on it. Her name is Svenrietta, and she is a registered service animal. If found, please call the Cook family at 555-555-9213 anytime, day or night.

CHAPTER 11

Broken

Told by Manda

It's supposed to be an expression. Hearts are muscle, not bone. They can't *actually* break. But, when Svenrietta disappeared, I swear, my brother's heart shattered. She'd been making Shady a little stronger and braver every day, and once she was gone, he folded inward and crumbled like a dying leaf.

Shady wouldn't eat. He couldn't sleep. He refused to go to his appointments with his psychiatrist. He wouldn't even go to school. And—worst of all—for the first time ever, he completely stopped talking. Even to me, Mom, and Dad.

Mom moved some meetings around on Tuesday. Dad

worked from home on Wednesday, but by the time Thursday came, they couldn't do it anymore.

"Shady, you *need* to get dressed," I heard Mom plead that morning.

I peered in the doorway to see a tight lump of covers on my brother's bed.

"Just give school a try. If you really can't cope, Dad or I will come to get you." The blanket lump didn't move.

Mom tried a threat. "I'm coming back in five minutes," she said, "and you'd better be up."

But, really, what was she going to do if he wasn't? Send him to his room? He was already there. Ban him from playing *The Evil Undead*? He mostly liked playing it with Pouya, and since he wouldn't even come out of his room to see his best friend, Pou had to go to the after-school program.

Mom walked out of Shady's room like she meant business, but when I went in to borrow a pair of socks from her drawer a minute later, I found her sitting on the edge of the bed crying. She didn't even try to stop when she saw me—so I knew it was bad. I sat down and put an arm around her.

"I can stay home with him today if you want," I offered. "Most of my teachers post the assignments online anyway."

For some reason, that made her cry harder.

Dad came in. "I'm calling Dr. Nugget," he said when he saw my mom's runny mascara. "We can't go on like this."

While Dad spoke to the psychiatrist's receptionist on the phone, Mom seemed to rally. She put on earrings. She picked out shoes. Finally, with a callback from Shady's psychiatrist coming on Dad's cell within the hour, my parents decided there wasn't any other choice. Mom had important meetings. Dad couldn't miss another day with his big conference coming up. They weren't happy about it, but they asked me to stay home with my brother. They also decided he wasn't in any shape for Angie Murray to come babysit, even though I was supposed to have Film Fanatics after school. I said it was okay. And, honestly, I didn't mind at first.

Only, the silence was so much louder than I expected.

At first, I left Shady alone while I did some history homework. It was nice having the house to myself.

But when eleven thirty came around and he still hadn't come down for breakfast, I started to worry. I put a blueberry muffin on a plate and brought it to him. We're not allowed to eat in our rooms, so I figured he'd be happy.

Shady was still under his blanket, but at least now his head was poking out a little, and he had a comic book propped up in front of him.

I sat down on the edge of his bed. "Hey, you hungry?"

He shifted one shoulder away from me and stared harder at his comic.

"It's forbidden bedroom food." I smiled and held up the plate. "Don't tell Mom," I added as if everything was normal. As if he *could* tell Mom. I mean, at that point I half hoped he *would* tell her and get me in trouble because at least then he'd be talking.

"Come on. Try a bit?" I tugged at Shady's blanket playfully, but that only made him curl up tighter.

My phone buzzed.

Library. U coming?

It was Pascale. I hadn't forgotten that I was supposed to meet her at lunch. I'd even borrowed a scarf from my mom with little violets on it, and I was planning to ask her how to knot it.

I'd been working on a message all morning, but I kept

rereading it and hesitating to hit Send: *I'm SO sorry. Can't come today. Shady needs me at home. Still really upset about Svenri. Won't talk to anyone or come out of his room. Pls don't be mad, ok? Because I really, really, really want to be your friend!*

Nope.

Delete.

I mean, way to sound totally desperate!

Instead, I went with short and to the point.

Sorry. Can't. Tomorrow?

I watched the phone anxiously as the three little "I'm answering" dots appeared. Finally, it buzzed with her reply.

Sure.

One word.

I felt myself deflate. She was definitely mad. Which was great, because—as predicted—when I'd told Carly and Beth that I wasn't going to be in their film contest group anymore, they were all like, "Oh, okay. Fine. Whatever. No, really. It's *fine*." And ever since then they'd been acting like I no longer existed, right down to staring at their phones and pretending they didn't see me standing directly behind them in the lunch line. So now I had zero friends.

The phone buzzed again.

We can still edit after school tho? At film club?

At first, I didn't get what Pascale meant. Svenrietta was gone. Pascale had been there when she disappeared. You can't film a duckumentary without a duck. We had the school stuff, but we'd been planning to film Svenri at home with Shady next. We still didn't have enough footage to meet the minimum ten-minute run time for the film. Why bother editing?

She must have guessed what I was thinking.

Now we film about the absence of the duck.

I glanced at the defeated lump of covers on the bed. *That* was the absence of the duck. And it wasn't fit to be filmed.

"Shady," I tried softly, holding out the muffin again. "It's blueberry. Your favorite."

No response.

"Fine then." I took a bite. "Mmmm," I said in an exaggerated way. "So good."

Shady looked right through me with the same blank stare he gives to waiters, the dentist, and the lady at the flower shop who always tries to get him to say hello.

I sighed.

Sorry. We have to cancel the movie. My brother is too upset.

The three dots appeared.

But that's part of the story! It's documentary. Whatever happens, you film it.

I blinked at my phone, not knowing what to say. I mean, sure. Telling what happens is what documentaries do. But my brother's broken heart wasn't just some story for people's entertainment.

"You sure you don't want some?" I nudged the blanket lump.

Silence. He closed his eyes.

My phone buzzed again.

If he's too sad now, we can edit the first half, then pick up filming later. No big deal.

Only, it *was* a big deal. It was a very big deal. Ever since my brother stopped talking in kindergarten, he'd been taking the tiniest baby steps toward communicating. A small smile for our favorite aunt, a little wave to thank the postal worker who'd just brought him a birthday package. Then Svenri came along and changed everything. And now that she was gone, he was right back where he'd started—only worse, because at least in kindergarten he hadn't been miserable like this. My brother couldn't handle a camera in his face. Definitely not now. Maybe not ever.

You don't get it. He isn't going to feel better without Svenri.

Then I made a snap decision that wasn't snap at all. It was inevitable, really. I'd been kidding myself for months thinking I could do this.

I need to quit film club.

There was a long pause as my screen stayed blank, then—

Swell

I didn't need to hear Pascale say it. Just reading it, I could feel the sarcasm dripping off that single word. I could picture her perfect nose turned up in the air, the stormy look in her dark eyes. I'd ruined our project and her chance to go to New Orleans. She was going to hate me forever. *Swell.* Just swell.

"Okay, Shady. Fine." I took another bite of the muffin. It tasted like sawdust. "Fine," I said with my mouth full. "If you don't want it, don't eat it."

My brother had opened his eyes again. He was watching me with his deer-in-the-headlights look.

The phone buzzed.

Now I know your commitment to filmmaking.

I wanted to scream. First, at Pascale: "You don't know the first thing about commitment. You don't have a brother like Shady!"

Second, at my parents: "Why did you make me join film club in the first place? I *knew* something like this would happen."

Last, I wanted to scream at the entire world. For being the kind of place that makes a person like Shady so uncomfortable and overwhelmed in the first place. For not even trying to learn how to make him feel okay.

Mostly, though, I felt like screaming at myself. Like: "Why can't you find a way to make him better? What kind of big sister are you?" and also "How could you be so stupid? You almost had a real friend who liked you for who you are, and now you've messed it up by acting all weird. Like always!"

But the one person I ended up screaming at was the one who didn't deserve it.

"Just so you know," I told Shady. "It's film club day. My one day of the week to do my own stuff after school instead of looking after you, but I'll be here instead. I don't know if you've noticed, but everything is always about you."

I scrunched my hand around the remaining muffin, squashing it into a ball.

"Shady doesn't like noise, so we can't go to the water park. Shady gets anxious around people he doesn't know. Never mind, we'll skip the Christmas party at the Marshalls' house where you make gingerbread houses and get to take them home."

His eyes were wider now. Glassier. But he still didn't react, which made me even angrier.

"Shady lost his duck. He won't get out of bed, so Angie can't come babysit," I went on.

Silence.

"That's it?" I asked. "You've still got nothing to say? Why don't you just talk?" I yelled. "Why don't you just get over yourself and talk?"

Something in me snapped. I threw the muffin ball at my brother—hard enough that it exploded into chunks and crumbs when it hit the duvet. Shady looked down at the mess, then he pulled the blanket over his shoulder and turned to face the wall. Muffin crumbs tumbled to the carpet.

"Oh my God!" I yelled. Then I left, slamming the door behind me. But by the time I got downstairs I was already regretting every word. I collapsed on the bottom step—tears streaming down my face.

Let's All Get into the Holiday Spirit!

Family and friends are invited to join us in the gymnasium on Tuesday, December 23, for a holiday show, *Santa's Tree Trouble*. (Note: Kindergartners will be participating in a separate show.) Seating is available on a first-come, first-served basis.

If possible, please bring a donation of peanut butter, pasta, baby diapers, or unexpired canned goods for the food pantry or a toy for the Inner City Kids' toy drive. (Toys should be new, unwrapped, and unopened.) We'll have bins set up outside the doors. There will be door-prize tickets given for all donations. Photography is allowed, and there will also be time for pictures in costume following the show.

Doors open at 6:45.

Show begins at 7:00.

CHAPTER 12

Lunch Lady

Told by Pouya

The day Shady finally came back to school, things went bad fast. To begin with, he wasn't talking to me. That might sound normal, since Shady never talks to me. But I mean he wasn't even *not talking* to me in the usual ways.

"Hey," I said when I met him by the coat hooks. "You're back. Okay. Here's what you missed."

I'd been keeping a list in my head—not of homework or spelling words, just stuff I knew he'd like—and there was lots. We hadn't seen each other in almost four days.

"The first day you were gone, Shushanna got hit in the head with a dodgeball, and it knocked one of her teeth out.

It was loose already. But still..."

This wasn't huge news. Somebody got hit in the head with a dodgeball at least twice a week, but I wasn't about to lead with my biggest story. Normally, Shady would have asked a question with his eyebrows or by shrugging his shoulders. Like, *Was there blood? How much?* He didn't, so I told him anyway.

I cupped my hands, then parted them to demonstrate how the blood had spilled through Shushanna's fingers. "Blood everywhere. Mr. Nelson had to bring out the puke mop."

Shady stared straight ahead.

I pressed on. "Also, I've been working on our Bar Graph of Butt." I dug around in my backpack to find it. "Tuesday was a huge butt day. See?" I held up the paper he and I had been working on since October. Basically, we used little check marks to record the number of times Mrs. Okah said the word *but* during class.

For example: "Open your math books, but don't start the problems yet." We'd look across the room, smirk at each other, then make a check mark. At the end of the day we compared butt numbers, took the average, and plotted it on our graph. The beauty of it was that if we ever got caught, I could say it was educational.

Shady gave me a blank look.

So I brought out the most important news. "And the Apocalypse Preparedness Squad is doing great. We got some fourth graders to join. One of them is Jang Hu."

I waited for Shady to look impressed, but he didn't look anything at all.

"Her family owns Hu's Convenience Store."

Still nothing.

"Just think of all the canned goods she has access to!"

This was lifesaving information. According to the latest internet reports, Planet Q was still on course to crash into Earth on December 31, and when Gavin's cat, Raven, had given birth to an entire litter of pure-white kittens, the final sign—*The color shall be bleached from the creatures before the sun rises for the last time*—had come to pass! Now, obviously, if Planet Q made direct contact with North America, we'd all be exploded, and canned fruit wasn't going to help, but if it happened to hit another continent instead, having the right supplies could mean the difference between survival and certain death.

Shady didn't look at all relieved though.

"Hey, Shady." Tamille was standing behind us with her

fingers hooked under her backpack straps. "Did you find your duck yet?"

Shady looked down. He started grinding the heel of one shoe against the floor.

"Not yet." I answered for him, so she'd go away. But she didn't.

Of course, I'd been looking everywhere for Svenri. Lots of kids had. Students had combed every inch of the school-yard for days.

I'd even considered the possibility of foul play in her disappearance. First, I confronted Matt D. and Jeremiah, the two fifth graders who'd kicked in a snowman the Friday before she vanished. I figured they'd have a motive, since we'd gotten in their way and defended the underducks (a couple little kids who'd only been trying to enjoy the first packing snow of the year). They swore they were at a basketball tournament when she disappeared though, and their story checked out with Mr. Sadako, the gym teacher. My only other suspects were Pearl Summers (who hated Svenrietta with a passion) and her evil friends Monica and Rebecca, but they were all in the holiday play, and they'd been standing with me on the stage when it happened. They couldn't have done it.

"I made you a card." Tamille pulled a folded paper out of her backpack and tried to hand it to Shady, but he just stood there with his arms at his sides.

Obviously, it wasn't the first time I'd seen Shady so upset that he'd shut down. It happened sometimes, like after this fifth grader named Carl came right up to his face and yelled, "Are you deaf?" Or on pajama days when he just dressed regular (because wearing pajamas makes people look at him, and he hates that) and kids bugged him about it. Or the time Mark complained to the teacher because he didn't want to do group work with Shady because he never contributes to the discussion.

I'd never seen Shady quite this bad though.

"Thanks," I said, taking the card from Tamille. It was glittery. The front said *Sorry about your duk*. "Come on, Shady." He followed me into class, but as soon as he sat down, kids crowded around.

"Sucks about your duck," Connor said with a shrug.

"My mom thinks maybe it just flew south," Angela told him. "So, it might come back in the spring. Don't give up, okay?"

"I miss Duck Tales reading club," Tammy added. "Mrs.

Patton brought a big dog stuffed animal to read to and changed the name to Dog Tales. But now it's just stupid."

Shady's face was red. His shoulders were tight. He was hating every minute of this.

"Well, at least there aren't feathers all over the classroom anymore," Pearl said. For once, nobody agreed with her.

I could tell Shady was relieved when the national anthem came on, and then Mrs. Okah jumped straight into a math unit about 3-D shapes.

I saw her glance in Shady's direction a few times as she talked, but she answered for him when she called attendance (instead of getting him to raise his hand like she'd been doing lately), and she knew enough not ask him any yes-or-no questions about prisms and spheres.

The *real* trouble happened at lunch.

As soon as the bell rang, I dragged my chair over to Shady's desk to keep him company and hopefully to keep other kids from reminding him about Svenrietta—like either of us needed reminding!

"A lavash wrap," I said sadly as I opened my lunch. I didn't have to explain it to Shady. I knew he remembered. Lavash was the same bread I'd used that first day to lure

Svenri into my backpack when she was just a duckling. I couldn't bring myself to eat it, but I took a bite of a celery stick. Shady, on the other hand, didn't bother to take out his lunch bag at all, which was why he was just sitting there with an empty space in front of him when the substitute lunch monitor came in.

She had flat gray hair, pale veiny skin, and ankles like tree trunks. I'd never seen her before, but she was wearing the red vest with the picture of an apple on it that all lunch monitors wear. Obviously, she was filling in for our regular monitor, Mrs. Bolhuis. But this lady had none of Mrs. Bolhuis's knock-knock jokes or charm.

"You there. In the red shirt. Get down and pipe down," she snapped at Connor, who'd been standing on his chair, yelling across the room for Gavin to open the window so he could try to throw grapes out it. "If I see any food being tossed, the tosser will be in the office so fast their head will spin."

She pointed at a granola bar wrapper on the floor and used the fury in her eyes to make Jasmin pick it up. It looked like she was about to rain terror on another room, but she stopped, pivoted, and headed straight for us.

"Did you forget your lunch at home?" she asked Shady.

"I think he's just not hungry," I answered.

"He's got a tongue! He can answer for himself." The lunch lady tilted her head and stood there, staring Shady down.

"He doesn't," I explained.

"Doesn't have a tongue?"

"Doesn't talk," I said.

"Isn't this a fifth-grade class?" She pointed at the bulletin board, where Mrs. Okah posted the monthly calendar and spelling words. It clearly said at the top *Room 9: 5th Grade*, so I didn't think she wanted an answer. "By the fifth grade you should be more than capable of answering when spoken to," she told Shady. "Kindergarten babies can do that much!"

"He actually can't," Pearl said with a little smile, which, I think, is what really set Tree Trunks off.

"Oh, I see," she answered, looking around the classroom. "You've got a substitute lunch lady, so you think you can pull a fast one. Well, I wasn't born yesterday."

I don't know what made me say it. Maybe it was a combination of really hating her and really wanting to distract her from Shady.

"Uh...yeah," I said. "Because you were born a hundred years ago."

A bunch of kids laughed.

"Office!" She pointed to the door. Next, she zeroed in on Shady. "You too. Maybe you can find your tongue and explain to the principal why you don't have an ounce of respect."

As she said this, she reached down and plucked off his sunglasses. "You don't need these inside." She dropped them on the teacher's desk.

Suddenly exposed to the room, Shady blinked fast and cowered in his chair like a trapped animal.

"You can't send him to the office for not doing something he can't do, stupid!" I said. "And he's allowed to wear sunglasses if he wants to."

"Watch. Your. Language. Young man." The lunch lady's voice was low and growly.

"It's true," DuShawn said. He smoothed out his skirt nervously. His voice was shaking a little, but he seemed determined to help. "Shady is allowed to wear sunglasses. And he doesn't talk."

"He never talks," Arjana put in. "And you're not supposed to force him."

But the lunch lady wasn't listening to anyone. She jabbed her finger toward me in the air.

"To the office. Now."

"You'll regret this," I said, getting to my feet. I knew once I explained what had happened to Mrs. Mackie, Tree Trunks would be in trouble, not us. "Come on," I said. But when I turned back, expecting Shady to be following me, he was still in his seat. And his whole body was shaking.

"Oh my God!" Pearl Summers yelled. "What's wrong with him?" Everyone turned to look, which made Shady shake harder.

He started crying. Big, silent tears slipped down his cheeks. He had his arms hugged across his body, but they were vibrating madly too. So were his legs. He'd broken out in sweat on his forehead.

I'd seen it before—but only once. This time his mom took us to the trampoline gym in second grade. Big kids were pushing, and the music was way, *way* too loud.

"He's having a panic attack," I said. "Someone go get a teacher."

"Nobody leaves this room," the lunch lady thundered.

DuShawn and Arjana were already getting out of their

seats. Then Jackson got up to help too. But to my surprise, of all people, Pearl Summers was the first one to reach the door. "It's okay, Shady," she said over her shoulder. "I'll be right back."

CHAPTER 13

Ducknapper

Told by Pearl Summers

I've seen horrible things in my life. A flattened cat at the side of the road. A waterfall of blood after Shushanna got her tooth knocked out in gym class. The time my cousin got stung on her eyelid by a wasp, and it swelled shut to the size of a baseball. But none of those things compared to what happened to Shady...because who knows who ran over the cat, Gavin threw the dodgeball that hit Shushanna, and the wasp sting was obviously the wasp's fault. But Shady's panic attack—that was because of me.

After Shady's mom came and helped him out to the car, the day mostly went back to normal, but I couldn't stop picturing his body vibrating like it was about to explode. I didn't even stay to do the final count of CandyGram money with Rebecca and Monica. When the bell rang, I ran home to make things right—only, as hard as I tried, things only went more wrong.

As soon as I got inside, Juliette started whining and yapping.

Yip, yip, yip.

She danced around me, then ran down the hall to the door that connects to our garage. She scratched at it with her front paws, then ran back.

Yip, yip, yip.

She circled and did the same routine again.

"Shhhhhh," I scolded. Juliette followed me down the hall toward the garage door. On my way past, I reached up and carefully reaffixed the sign that was coming loose. *Stay out. Plant Isolation Music Experiment in Progress.* The playlist I'd set up on my laptop was blaring. Good. I just needed to deal with Juliette, and then I could do what needed to be done.

"Come on," I said. "Outside, then peanut butter."

Outside and *peanut butter* are my dog's favorite words,

and as soon as I said them, she trotted at my side with only the odd yap. I opened the back door, and she went out. Then I started preparing a mega-sandwich: four slices of bread piled one on top of the other with jam in between each piece.

After I'd called my mom to let her know I was home safe, I filled Juliette's chew toy with organic peanut butter. When I let her in, she went straight to work licking it, and I was able to sneak away to the garage.

"It's me," I called over the music, but I didn't even have to say it. Yes, she was disruptive, loud, totally stinky, and extremely messy, but she was also almost as smart as Juliette. The second Svenrietta heard the doorknob turning, she knew it was mega-sandwich time.

Wak. Wak. Wak.

Svenrietta waddled over, looked up, and waited obediently.

Wait, right? What was the duck doing in my garage?

Trust me. I'd been asking myself the same thing for the last four days. I *hated* that duck. And when she disappeared, if you'll remember, I was standing at the front of the gym as Elfina, about to sing my solo. There were tons of witnesses in the room who could swear it wasn't even physically possible for me to steal the duck!

But I did.

The day Svenrietta went missing, the whole school was searching for her. Kids walked the schoolyard calling her name. Mr. Nelson checked every broom closet. Mr. Sadako crawled under the stage with a flashlight. Mrs. Mackie put out an announcement for all of us to look behind our coats and in our cubbies. Every single person wanted to find Svenrietta, except me—so, of course, I was the unlucky one.

Dad was picking me up because I had lots of stuff to bring home. Specifically, the boxes that needed to be wrapped to look like presents for the holiday musical. I'd offered to do it because I'm a good present wrapper, and, as the Sock Ball/Suck Ball banner disaster proved, you can't leave these things to just anyone if you want them done right.

Most of the boxes, which were piled at the back of the gym, were still collapsed, but they were stacked inside one that wasn't. And when I lifted it:

Wak!

I nearly dropped the box of boxes. I wish I had. If I'd left it there on the gym floor, someone else would have found her eventually. I mean, probably. Even once I knew she was in there, she was hard to spot. She'd nestled herself way into one corner, and her brown feathers blended with the cardboard.

And, yes, I could have taken her straight to the office to turn her in. But in that moment, I had this thought, which I'd been having for weeks: *Ducks don't belong at school*. Not only had she ruined my solo that day, but she was always getting feathers everywhere and disrupting class with her quacking. Plus—even with the diaper—she smelled. It wasn't her fault, exactly. She was a wild animal. She belonged outside! Which was exactly where I was going to put her. I just had to get her out of the building first.

That was easy. By hiding in the box, she'd practically done the job for me. I carried her to the car and put her in the trunk. It was only once we got home that things got complicated.

"I'm taking these to the backyard to shake the dust off them," I told my dad once he'd parked the car. He had a teleconference to do. He wasn't really paying attention, so it was easy enough to carry the boxes to the back deck to release the duck.

The only problem was, she refused to be released.

"There," I said, tipping the box gently onto one side. "Go free!"

Wak.

"Come on." I shook the box a little. "Now's your chance." She didn't budge, so I took a deep breath and reached in. "Ouch!" She bit me. Well, not *bit*-bit me. It was more of a nip. I couldn't even tell if she had teeth, really...but she definitely *beaked* me.

"Stupid duck!"

By then, Juliette had spotted me through the back door. She wanted to come out and play. She was barking her head off. It was only a matter of time before she disturbed my dad on his call, and he came to see why I wasn't letting her out.

"Okay. Enough," I told the duck. "Out!" I tipped the box almost upside down.

Wak, wak, wakwakwakwak.

Svenrietta was losing her mind—which seemed rude since I was only trying release her into her natural habitat, but as I righted the box, I heard a faint rolling noise. I looked in, and then I understood.

"Oh."

A big grayish-white egg had come to rest in one corner.

Yes, Svenrietta had bitten/beaked me. But it was because she'd been protecting her baby!

"Oh," I said again, this time with dread. I'd seen eggs hatch at an exhibit at the science museum. It happened inside a plastic dome that was temperature-controlled because the eggs and chicks needed to stay warm.

It was December. There were, like, three feet of snow in the yard. Setting Svenrietta free in the wild was one thing. She had feathers. She'd fly away and make a nest or something. She'd be fine. But if I set her egg free, too, it would freeze. And that was one big step up from ducknapping. That was duck *murder*.

I had to think fast—which is where the idea for the plant experiment in the garage came in. I wasn't even exactly lying. I *was* planning to do an experiment for the science fair—*Do* plants grow better when you play them Beyoncé twenty-four hours a day?—and it was a great way to keep my parents out of the garage. (Isolation was my control factor.) Most importantly, the music helped to drown out the duck sounds, because Svenrietta *wasn't* quiet.

At first, it was only going to be for one night. My plan was to drop an anonymous note on Shady's desk, telling him where and when to find her, then leave her and her egg in a safe spot—but he didn't show up at school the next day, or the one after that, or the one after that.

"Sit, Svenri." I did the hand motion I'd seen Shady do. I tore off a piece of mega-sandwich. She waited until I threw it, then caught it midair in her beak.

"How's Aggie today?"

While Svenrietta ate, I walked over to check. The nest she'd built for her egg was mostly made of shredded newspaper and strips of cardboard she'd pulled off some old boxes. It was nestled inside one end of my parents' two-person kayak—nice and warm.

And okay, I know. *Aggie?* Yes, I'd named the egg. But it was hard not to get attached to both of them. Svenrietta was a good mom—always going right back to the nest after she ate. And I liked the way she closed her eyes and her whole body seemed to relax when I petted her.

I knew I couldn't keep them any longer though. Not after Shady's panic attack. Svenrietta had to go home. He needed her.

My new plan was simple. Mom wouldn't be home for another hour. That was plenty of time to put on some gardening gloves, scoop Svenrietta's nest and Aggie into a box, wrap some old towels around them for warmth, walk the two blocks to Shady's house, put the box on the doorstep, then ring the bell and wait in the bushes to make sure someone answered and took them in.

It would have been as easy as that, too, if it wasn't for the sudden, frantic scratching at the door.

Yip. Yip. Yip, yip, yip.

Juliette had finished her peanut butter. Her doggy senses had been telling her for days that there was a duck in the garage, and she was desperate to get in. Of course, I wasn't going to let her, only…

YIP, YIP, YIP.

The barking got louder, nearly drowning out Beyoncé. Before I knew what was happening, Juliette was inside. I must have left the door unlatched when I'd come in! Total disaster!

"Stop, Juliette!" I yelled as she raced toward Svenri. "No! Bad dog!" I tried to grab her, but she was already nipping at Svenrietta's tail feathers. The duck flapped her wings frantically and landed on some boxes, just out of Juliette's reach. For a second, I thought everything was going to be okay, but then she flapped again and went even higher, up into the loft space of the garage where my parents store lawn chairs, the patio umbrella, and other stuff we don't need until spring.

"Get out, Juliette!" I grabbed my dog and put her back in the house, but by then it was too late. Svenrietta had waddled to the back of the loft.

I dragged a storage container over and stood on top so I could see her.

"Here, ducky, ducky." I put a piece of sandwich down at the edge of the loft, but she was too freaked out to come get it. Her feathers were quivering. She was panting.

I searched the garage for something I could climb up on, but even standing on two big containers didn't get me high enough to swing my leg up, plus it was tippy—then...

"You in there, sweetie?"

I nearly toppled off my tower of containers.

My dad had been away on a business trip. I wasn't expecting him home that early.

"Don't come in!" I yelled. "It'll wreck the plant experiment."

"Okay," he said. "But meet me in the living room when you're done. I have a surprise for you."

I left some bread and a dish of water on the ledge for Svenrietta, then dragged the big containers back to their spots. My dad always brought good stuff home from his trips. Last time it was a pair of bedazzled noise-canceling headphones he found at the Dallas airport. "I'll be back to check on you later," I said softly to Svenrietta.

It wasn't until I had my hand on the doorknob that I remembered: Aggie!

If Svenrietta was too scared to come down to take care of her egg, what would happen to it? The temperature wasn't freezing in our garage, but it wasn't exactly warm either.

I walked over to the kayak and peered inside. "Okay, Aggie," I said. "I guess you're coming with me." I put the egg in the front pocket of my sweatshirt and wrapped one hand around it to keep it warm. Then I went to see what Dad had bought me.

CHAPTER 14

Tree Trouble

Told by Pouya

With one day to go before the opening night of *Santa's Tree Trouble*, Mrs. Carlisle made a truly terrible directing decision.

"That's it, Pouya!" she yelled at me. "You're out of the play!"

I'll admit, maybe I'd been hogging the stage a little—but it was only because I was still trying to fully explore the role of the tree.

"Why *can't* it be a juggling tree?" I said as I picked up the last of the three ornaments I'd just dropped. One of them was a bit smashed.

"Because it's just not," Mrs. Carlisle answered with a sigh. "It's also not a yodeling tree or a tap-dancing tree or a cross-eyed tree with its tongue sticking out. But, more importantly, you're being disruptive and disrespectful to the other actors."

"Totally." Pearl Summers tapped one curly elf shoe. The shoes were the only part of her costume she was wearing for dress rehearsal, but Mrs. Carlisle never said how *that* was being disrespectful to the other actors.

Connor was sweating buckets in his Santa suit and beard. Every other elf was in red-and-green tights and shirts with bells, and I was holding my branches. But Pearl had on a big bulky sweater with a zipper at the front, and she was carrying a shiny purse that she'd bragged her dad had bought her in New York. She had it tucked under her sweater, and she wouldn't let anyone touch it. I'd even heard her yell at Rebecca that it was private when she asked what was inside.

"I've been saying for weeks now that he's *so* disrespectful," Pearl went on.

"Pearl." Mrs. Carlisle shot her a *shhhhh* look.

Disrespectful. There was that word again. The same one Mrs. Mackie used the day when I stood up to the evil lunch lady. But I'm all about respect! I mean, there's a difference between being disrespectful and taking action when things aren't right. Isn't there? My moms showed me that when we left Iran (a country where it's against the law for two ladies to be in love) to make a new life someplace we can live freely.

And it's like Shady and I promised to do: make Carleton Elementary a safe place for the underducks. If anyone was an underduck, it was Shady. But now it was my turn. And I was going to have to stand up for myself.

"You're being dumb!" I yelled at Mrs. Carlisle. I waved my script around. "It doesn't say anywhere what kind of tree it's supposed to be. That's up to the actor. It's called creative expression! Plus, the play is tomorrow. How are you going to find a new tree in time?"

Here's an important lesson: never call a teacher dumb, even if that teacher is being dumb.

Mrs. Carlisle pointed in the direction of the office. Then, before I'd even left the stage: "Hayden," she called to one of the reindeer who didn't have a speaking part. "Congratulations. You're our new tree."

Hayden? Really? We used to be in Friends of the Environment club together. He'd once upcycled an empty tissue box into a new tissue box by putting different tissue in it. Hayden was nice and everything, but he was about as creative as a rock! The role of the tree needed so much more—even if I didn't know exactly what that was yet.

"All you have to say is, 'Do you think Santa might like a Christmas tree?'" Mrs. Carlisle instructed Hayden as I threw my branches down and stomped out of the gym. "Nice and loud, okay? I'll cue you."

By the time I got to the office, I was furious, so furious that Mrs. Mackie didn't even bother giving me detention. She was nice to me, which made me even madder.

"It's been a hard week for you, hasn't it, Pouya?" she said. "Especially now that Shady won't be coming back to school. I think losing the role of the tree is enough of a consequence. You can go back to class. But I want you to remember to be respectful to teachers and other staff members. Even when you disagree with them, okay?"

I did *not* agree to that, but she let me go anyway.

I fumed through the rest of the day, refusing to answer questions in geography and shoving past Pearl when she got in my way near the gym doors. "Watch it!" she yelled, throwing her arms up and pushing me back to protect her precious secret purse. "You almost broke it!"

"It's just an ugly purse!" I shouted, but she ignored me, then went straight over to complain that she had a headache so that she could sit out during dodgeball.

I was still mad when it was time to go to Shady's place. (Since he was being homeschooled now, his mom wanted him to have social interaction at least once a day, and I was invited back over.) Manda came to pick me up. That was because the Banana Bandit was still prowling the streets in his hairy gorilla costume, and Shady's mom said no walking alone. Luckily, Manda was in a terrible mood too. She and I barely talked on the way there. And even though Shady and Manda's mom welcomed me at the door and offered me a fresh-baked cookie, I barely mumbled thanks.

"I'm glad you're here, Pouya," she said with a smile. "Shady will be so happy to see you."

But, when I went upstairs, my best friend didn't seem happy to see me. He didn't seem happy at all, which—actually—was a relief, because I was in no mood for happiness.

"I hate Mrs. Carlisle." I dropped my backpack on the floor. "And I hate Mrs. Mackie even more. I hate that whole school. I'm glad it's probably going to blow up in ten days along with the rest of the world. You're lucky you don't have to go there anymore."

Shady was watching a movie on his laptop. Something

about invading space aliens that wasn't even educational. He just stared straight ahead.

Okay, maybe I shouldn't have said that he was lucky. I would have given anything to get to stay home too. Nobody teasing you about the weird-smelling (but delicious) kebabs in your lunch, no getting up to walk to school in the cold, no Pearl Summers. Sign me up! But I guess when it isn't your choice, it probably doesn't feel so great.

"Sorry," I grumbled. I figured I should explain what had happened. "I'm just mad because Mrs. Carlisle cut me out of the play." I dug around in my backpack for my script, then crumpled it up and threw it toward Shady's trash can—only I missed, and it landed on the floor. "I'm not allowed to be the tree anymore. She gave it to Hayden. Hayden! Have you ever met anyone who'd make a less inspiring tree?"

Shady lowered the volume on his laptop, so I knew he was listening.

"All because I was trying to make the role bigger and better. You know, give people one last great show before the world ends." I picked up the script, took a few steps back, and tried to throw it again. I missed again. "She said I was being disrespectful."

I picked up the script. Threw. Missed.

"Dammit!"

I don't know why. Of all the terrible things that had happened in the last few days, that dumb script was what finally put me over the edge.

Instead of tossing it toward the trash a fourth time, I hurled it at the wall above Shady's desk. It bounced off and fell to the floor uselessly. Then I lay down on his bed and started to cry.

I hate crying, but if you have to cry, Shady's room is a good place to do it. For one thing, it's dark. The door is always closed, and the curtains are usually pulled. The bed is soft, with a thick duvet. His mom buys Kleenex with lotion, and Shady's not about to tell anyone you sobbed like a baby.

The last two times I'd cried were in his room—first because my grandmother, Mamani, died in Iran and I never got to say goodbye, and another time because I failed math, and I knew Maman and Mitra-Joon were going to kill me. Both times, Shady just sat there playing the *Evil Undead* while he waited for me to finish, which is exactly what a best friend should do.

This time was no different. At least, not at first. While I buried my face in his pillow, Shady stayed at his desk, working on something. I could hear the *scratch-scratch-scratch* of his pencil against a paper, same as he always does in class when he's bored or nervous. And a few minutes later, he sat down beside me and tapped me on the shoulder.

Look, he said with his eyes.

He handed me the crumpled script I'd thrown at his wall:

SCRIPT: SANTA'S TREE TROUBLE
©Dolly Shannon, 2015

CAST OF CHARACTERS

Tree ....A scraggly old pine tree that wants
to be included in Christmas

Santa .... The jolly old man himself

Mary Claus ....Santa's wife

Elfina .... Santa's head elf

Earl the elf .... Mischievous elf 1

Elvira the elf .... Mischievous elf 2

Elvis the elf .... Mischievous elf 3

Snowman..........................A wise old snowman

Narrator 1

Narrator 2

Narrator 3

SETTING AND SCENES

SCENE 1: Outside the toy workshop at the North Pole, with fake snow and fake evergreens.

SCENE 2: Inside the toy workshop, with benches for toy making.

SCENE 3: In the forest. Fake snow, fake evergreens.

SCENE 4: Back outside the toy workshop. (see Scene 1)

SCENE 5: In the forest (see Scene 3) but with a nighttime sky backdrop.

SCENE 6: Back inside the toy workshop. (see Scene 2)

PROPS

- Fake ax
- Four large, brightly wrapped cardboard boxes
- Plate of bright, perfectly decorated Christmas cookies
- Various toys
- Various toy-building tools
- Christmas decorations and garlands
- Large, star-shaped tree topper

APPROXIMATE RUNNING TIME: 30–35 minutes, not including songs from the chorus.

"It's like what you made in the sensory room," I said, remembering the poster with sticky notes. "Is it a poem?"

He tilted one hand: *so-so*.

It was the most he'd talked to me since Svenrietta had disappeared.

"Is this always what you're doing when you scribble on paper?"

He nodded.

"'Troubled characters that want to be included...'" I read from the start. "You mean me?"

Shady pointed at himself.

"You want to be in the play too?"

Another *so-so* hand.

I gave that some thought. Obviously, Shady didn't want a speaking part. At least, I didn't think so. But that didn't mean he didn't want to be included somehow. Even though it was hard to tell sometimes, he always wanted to be part of things. Who *wouldn't* want that?

"You want to be in the chorus?" I asked.

He made a face.

I made a face back.

The chorus is where they stick kids who aren't talented

enough to do anything else. Everyone knows that. But why did it have to be an onstage part (which always seem to go to the popular, outgoing kids) or the chorus? It felt unfair that there wasn't another option.

"Maybe we can think of a way," I said. "Can you tell me what you want to do in the play? Write it down or something?"

Shady answered with an awkward shrug. Now that I realized he was always making poems, I knew he liked writing... but scribbling away words was a different kind of writing. He never liked just saying his thoughts plainly on paper to answer questions.

"Personally, what I *really* want is to still be the tree," I said. "But not just any tree. I want to be a different tree, y'know? A kind of tree that makes the audience stop and think."

Shady leaped up and walked across the room. He scanned his bookshelf, looking for something specific. A second later, he pulled a book out and handed it to me.

ALLIGATOR PIE

Poems by Dennis Lee

"You think I should be an alligator tree?"

He took the book back, opened it, and ran his finger under some of the words. When that didn't help, he gave up and closed it again. He motioned for me to look, then lay one finger over part of the first line of text: ALLIGATOR PIE

"A?"

He nodded, then moved on to the next part: *Poems*

"Po-e," I read.

More nodding.

He went back to the alligator part, covering different let-ters with his fingers: ALLIGATOR

"T, R," I read.

He moved to another part: *by Dennis Lee*

"E, E."

It took me a second to put it all together. "A poetree?"

Shady nodded hard.

"You think I should be a poe-tree. Like, a tree that talks in poems?"

He grinned, then he pointed at himself, then back at me.

"You think we should *both* be the poetree!"

And that was it. We had it.

The play was going to be saved after all.

CHAPTER 15

Egg Exhaustion

Told by Pearl Summers

After my aunt Shannon had my baby cousin Mitzi last year, she looked like she'd been run over by a truck. She had dark circles under her eyes from not sleeping. She wore pajama pants with baby barf on them all day, and she pretty much never washed her hair anymore.

That was how I felt by the time the holiday play came around—minus the baby barf.

If you think looking after an egg sounds easy, think again. According to the internet, a duck egg needs to be kept warm (but not too warm) all the time. The ideal temperature is 99.5 degrees Fahrenheit—which is about body temperature—and keeping that temperature constant is critical to the duckling's survival.

Unless you happen to have an incubator, you need a mother duck to sit on the egg. And since the only duck I had was still refusing to come down from the garage loft, the only choice I had was to fill in for her. That meant keeping the egg warm with my body heat twenty-four hours a day. Not to mention keeping it safe, which is hard to do when your gym teacher expects you to play dodgeball, your best friend gets all hysterical because you won't tell her what's inside the purse you're suddenly carrying everywhere, and you're supposed to wear a skintight elf costume with no pockets to hide an egg in.

For four nights straight, I'd been up almost all night holding the egg. I was terrified I might roll over it if I fell asleep with it in my hand. I'd also been spending so much time in the garage trying to coax Svenrietta down that I hadn't practiced my solo for the show once. I needed that egg—and that duck—out of my life, so you can imagine my relief when I overheard Pouya telling Jang Hu that Shady was coming to watch the holiday musical with his parents.

Finally! Here was my chance to get the duck back to

him. The idea had come to me at the dress rehearsal when the other elves had used the props—those empty boxes I'd wrapped to look like presents. To sneak the duck back into the school, all I had to do was wrap her up like one of those fake gifts.

I could sneak it under Shady's seat where he'd be sure to find it. It would be like the ultimate Secret Santa gift. He'd be thrilled to have Svenrietta back, and—best of all— nobody would ever have to find out that I'd taken her. Plus, I'd put the egg in the box. Like a bonus present!

Everything was going according to plan too. I didn't feed Svenri breakfast that morning, so when I got home, she was starving. She came down right away to get her after-school mega-sandwich, and I scooped her into the box, tucking Aggie in gently underneath her, and wrapped them up like a present.

When it was time to get ready that night, I changed into my elf costume and put the duck box gently into the trunk of the car. And now that I was backstage, waiting for the show to start, all I had to do was keep a lookout to see where Shady and his family were going to sit so I could sneak over and deliver the duck-filled box.

"Where's my nose?!" Amber shrieked.

"On your face," Wendel answered.

"No, idiot. My reindeer nose. It was here a second ago."

"Who still needs makeup?" Mrs. Carlisle was running around with a brush and blusher. Anthony and Daryn tried to dodge her, but she caught up with them. "Boys too! This is stage makeup!"

I folded my elf hat in half and pressed it between my head and the wall like a pillow. If I could just get through this performance and get rid of the duck, I'd make it to winter break, and then I was going to sleep for two weeks solid.

I closed my eyes for just a second, then opened them to peer out into the audience. Just then, Gavin walked up behind me.

"Okay, I don't want to put pressure on anyone, but remember, this is probably going to be the last show these people ever see. So we need to make it great."

"I, for one, am planning to do my best performance," said Sara.

"Well, duh," Wendel said. "Nobody's going to do a bad job on purpose. It's not like we want to die with regrets."

"Oh, shut up!" I said. My head was aching. "If the world

is really ending on New Year's Day, I think people have big-ger problems than whether or not the school play is good." I—for one—definitely had bigger problems, like the fact that Shady and his family were still nowhere to be seen.

I sighed, peered out through the side of the curtain one more time, and caught sight of the glint of mirrored sun-glasses toward the back of the gym.

"Thank God." I glanced at the clock. Two minutes till showtime. I was going to have to move fast. "I need to—um—run to the art room and fix the tape on this box," I said to anyone who was listening, then I bent down to grab the present, but..."Where's my box?" I yelled.

"What box?" Sara asked.

"The one that was here a second ago!"

"It's probably with the rest of the props." She motioned toward stage left, where a big stack of present props—all identically wrapped—was sitting. Someone must have grabbed it in the split second I'd had my eyes closed.

"I need it!" I yelled. "I need it right now!"

"Everyone, places, please!" Mrs. Carlisle announced.

I thought for sure I was going to throw up.

CHAPTER 16

The Best Worst Play Ever

Told by Manda

I'd never seen our parents as proud as the day Shady asked to go see the school play.

It was the first time he'd talked to anyone in our family since Svenrietta went missing—so that was a relief for Mom and Dad—although he wasn't talking to me yet. I guess he was still mad about the muffin and the fit I'd thrown in his bedroom the week before. Every time I tried to apologize, he stared straight through me.

"This is so exciting," Mom said, settling into a plastic chair and looking around the gym in awe, like we were at a fancy opera. The fact that she'd barely left the house that week must have been affecting her brain. She was supposed to be homeschooling Shady, but I don't think she was cut out for it. Three times I'd come home and caught her staring wistfully at her briefcase while Shady played video games upstairs.

"Didn't the kids do a great job decorating the gym, Shady?" She pointed out a few sad paper snowflakes. "It looks like a winter wonderland in here. That must have been a fun art class." She all but winked at Dad. As I suspected, she was desperate for Shady to agree to go back to school after the holidays so she could go back to work.

If Shady caught her hint, he didn't react. Not that he'd usually talk to any of us anywhere near the school. (Someone might overhear.) But he didn't seem to have his usual vacant stare either. Instead, he was watching the front of the room intently, like he was excited for the play to start. I didn't want to burst his bubble, but based on the school's track record, it *wasn't* going to be outstanding. The music teacher, Mr. Consuela, always messed up the notes on the piano, and then there was the year Tabitha Shubert got so nervous that she threw up in Santa's sleigh.

"There are Lili and Mitra!" Dad said, waving Pouya's moms over to the two seats we'd saved for them.

Just then, the gym doors opened and about ninety kids dressed in red and green shuffled in and filled the spaces between the rows of benches in front of the stage: the chorus. Right away, cell phone cameras lit up.

"Oh, look!" Mom pointed to a spot on the far side of the gym. "There's Pouya." She stood up and waved. *So* embarrassing. "What's he doing in the chorus? I thought he was playing the Christmas tree. Isn't he the tree, Lili?" Mom asked, leaning across me and Shady to talk to her.

"I think so, yes," Lili answered, looking puzzled.

I glanced over. Was that the barest hint of a smile on Shady's face?

The lights went down. Mrs. Mackie stepped up to the microphone to welcome everyone. And then the best and worst Christmas play in Carleton Elementary history got underway.

It all began outside Santa's workshop.

"You guys!" Pearl Summers was standing center stage in a sparkly elf hat. She seemed kind of stunned, and for a second I thought she'd forgotten her next line, but then she blinked a few times and went on. "It's almost the most magical time of the year again."

"You mean reindeer games playoff season?" another elf answered with a corny wink. The audience laughed.

"No, silly! *Christmas*time," Pearl answered. The other elves on the stage made cheerful agreeing noises, and I tried not to roll my eyes. I didn't mean to be critical, but after watching so much classic cinema over the last few months, it was more obvious than ever that grade-school plays had rock-bottom standards.

My phone vibrated in my pocket, and I slid it out from under my program to check the text message—glad for something to pass the time.

I have an idea for another film. Not as great as the last, but pretty good. Come back to film club?

This was the first I'd heard from Pascale since last Thursday, when I'd told her we couldn't do a duckless duckumentary and that I was quitting the club. She'd since passed me twice in the halls without saying hello, and I'd honestly never expected to hear from her again. Between her ignoring me and Carly and Beth continuing to ghost me, I was basically resigned to my new lunch-hour routine of eating all alone then hanging out in the library doing homework. It was a quiet, lonely existence, but at least it was drama-free.

I hesitated a minute, then started typing.

Really sorry, but I'm not coming back. Shady needs me home after school. Even if I wanted to, I couldn't.

Before I could send it, I felt a short, sharp nudge on my arm. It was Shady.

"Shady's right, Manda," Mom whispered. "Put that away. It's rude to text during a performance."

I turned my phone off and tucked it under the program on my lap. By then, the kids in the chorus were singing a song about Christmas cheer—loudly and off key.

Mr. Consuela hit some very wrong notes, and half the kids got thrown off and forgot the words. I sighed. It was going to be a long hour. I was just starting to nod off when I felt Shady grab the concert program off my knee, and my phone along with it.

He propped the program up for cover from Mom's eyes, then started tapping the phone. I sighed at the unfairness but left him to it. He was obviously bored to death too. He was probably playing Woody Word Finder.

"Manda." Mitra was whispering my name, but I didn't hear her at first. Not until Lili tugged at my sleeve and pointed down the row. Mitra was holding up her cell phone. "I want to send video to Pouya's aunty, but my battery ran out," she whispered. "Can you?" She wiggled her dead phone back and forth. "And send to me?"

I nodded and took my phone back from Shady. At least it would give me something to do. The chorus had just finished their third holiday song—something about gifts from the heart—when I hit Record, and almost on cue, the commotion started at the front of the gym.

"Ouch!"

"Hey!"

"Excuse me." Pouya was standing on one of the chorus benches. "Excuse me. Coming through." I watched through my phone screen, keeping him in the center of the shot as he stepped over people, making his way to the stage.

Was this part of the play? Two of the reindeer had their mouths wide open, and Santa looked downright confused. Lili was leaning over, saying something to Mitra in Farsi. Meanwhile, Mrs. Carlisle was stepping forward like she was about to intervene.

Before she could stop him, though, Pouya hopped onto the stage and stood directly in front of the kid who'd been playing the tree. "Can I have those for a sec?" Without waiting for an answer, Pouya took the branches the kid had been holding and shoved them down the sleeves of his shirt so just the bushy green tips stuck out.

"A poem!" he announced loudly, facing the stunned audience. "Written by Shady Cook and recited by me, Pouya Fard."

Still holding the phone steady, I glanced over at Pou's moms. They looked as surprised as I was. Shady, meanwhile, was busy *tap-tap-tapping* one foot against the floor. His long hair flopped down, hiding his face.

"I am a tree. An old, gnarled tree," Pouya began. "So very green and prick-ely.

"And you might think that I'm not fit...for Santa's work-shop, 'cause I'm a bit..." He looked around at the audience. By now, Mrs. Carlisle was at the edge of the stage, giving him a death glare.

"Ugly...and weird...and dripping sap." Pouya pulled two little squirt bottles out of his back pockets, aimed them at the front row, and sprayed—I guess to symbolize tree sap?

Someone's grandma threw her hands up over her face, but a bunch of the little kids laughed.

"But wait a second!" Pouya yelled. "Look at that!"

He ran across the stage and retrieved something from behind the curtain. A huge, blinking, battery-powered star on a headband. He placed it on his head and returned to center stage.

"I have a light that shines so bright."

He grabbed two of the kids playing reindeer by the hand and launched them forward.

"It guides the reindeer through the night."

He paused dramatically.

"And also, as you plainly see…" Pouya gave a little bow as he finished up.

"I'm the world's most epic poe-tree."

There was a hush in the room that lasted several seconds. Then someone in the front row started clapping. The person next to them finally joined in, and eventually, it spread through the gym.

Meanwhile, Mrs. Carlisle was gesturing furiously at Pouya to get down from the stage. He didn't budge. Instead, he took another bow, then held one hand out toward the audience. "Shady Cook!" he said again. "The best poet in the fifth grade."

A few people sitting around us turned to look at my brother. I panned the cell phone camera over to catch his reaction. He was still looking down at the floor, but now I could see the corner of a smile through his hair.

Finally, after the applause died down, Pouya handed the branches back to their rightful owner and jumped off the stage, but nobody seemed to know what to do next.

"Pearl!" Mrs. Carlisle whispered loudly. Then she said it at full volume. "Pearl! Pick up from your next line." But Pearl Summers was standing at the front of the stage blinking like she couldn't quite remember where she was—let alone what she was supposed to be saying.

"Maybe this old tree is just what Santa needs after all," Mrs. Carlisle prompted, loud enough for the whole gym to hear.

"Maybe this old tree is just what Santa needs after all," Pearl repeated.

"Exactly!" a reindeer said. "It only needs a few finishing touches! And I know just the thing."

Most of the audience had settled down again, but some

of them were still watching Pouya, who was at the side of the room being told off by the principal in a hushed voice.

The reindeer walked across the stage toward a pile of presents. She picked one up off the top and started to carry it back.

"No! Wait!" Pearl yelled. "Don't give Santa that one!"

The boy who was playing Santa shot her a puzzled look, then grabbed the present from the reindeer anyway.

"I said! Not that one!" Pearl yelled even louder. "The one with the star is marked with an *X*. Look for the *X*, stupid! She grabbed hold of the box Santa was holding and tried to tug it away. "Connor! Give it to me *now*!" But Santa wouldn't let go.

"What are you doing?" he said through gritted teeth.

"Give. It. Here." Pearl pulled harder on the box. Finally, she managed to tug it out of Santa's hands, falling backward.

"Oof!" She fell on her butt. The box flew out of her hands and landed with a thud on the stage.

"You idiot!" Pearl yelled at Santa, as she scrambled onto her knees. "You might have killed them both!"

I zoomed in to get a better shot. This was a thousand

times more dramatic than any play Carleton Elementary had put on before.

Pearl was ripping furiously at the wrapping paper, throwing bits of it everywhere. She opened the flaps of the box, took a shuddering breath, and sank back on her heels. "Oh, thank God," she said. "They're in another one." Then she got up, walked over to the big pile of presents, and started lifting them up and shaking them gently, like an impatient kid on Christmas morning. The fourth box was the one that finally seemed to satisfy her. She ripped into the paper.

Meanwhile, the audience, now thoroughly confused, had started to shift in their seats and mutter to one another.

"She's here!" Pearl yelled. "They're both here. I think they're okay!"

Then all the kids on stage broke out in shouts as Pearl lifted a wriggling, flapping duck from the box.

Svenrietta!

Before my parents or I knew what was happening, Shady was on his feet, making his way down the row of crowded-in plastic chairs and straight to the front of the gym.

When Svenri caught sight of my brother, she went quackers. Pearl could hardly keep hold of her because her back end was wiggling madly. Shady climbed onto the stage and took her from Pearl's outstretched hands.

The duck buried her beak deep in my brother's armpit, her favorite place in the world. Meanwhile, he burrowed his face into her feathers, and they both stood there, oblivious to everyone around them as the gym broke into a flurry of confusion.

It was only because I was still zoomed in, filming the remarkable reunion between a boy and his duck, that I happened to notice Pearl Summers reach into the box behind Shady, take something else out, and run from the gym crying.

Then this popped up on my screen:

Great! So glad you're coming back. C U next Thursday.

What?! I hit End on the recording and scrolled back, looking for the message I'd written to Pascale—but hadn't gotten around to sending. *Had* I sent it by mistake? According to the phone, a message had gone through, but instead of the original—***Really sorry, but I'm not coming back. Shady needs me home after school. Even if I wanted to, I couldn't.***

I found this version where more than half of my words had been deleted:

I'm coming back. Shady needs me to.

I blinked at the screen as it hit me: maybe Shady wasn't mad about the muffin—maybe he was mad about me putting my life on hold for him. Maybe he didn't need me to. Maybe he didn't *want* me to. And, worse still, maybe all this time, as much as he'd been hiding behind me, I'd been hiding behind him too.

But by the time I looked up from the screen to try to find my brother, he was already gone.

CHAPTER 17

Cracked Open

Told by Pearl Summers

I know I'm not always nice. Two weeks ago, I told Erika Wallace her puffy winter jacket made her look like an Oompa Loompa (and then she stopped wearing it), but I only said it because it was nicer than mine. At ballet, I made three girls cry by suggesting that they shouldn't bother trying out for the lead in *Swan Lake Junior*. (But, seriously, Ashley's point is weak, and nobody was going to believe Clara or Sam in the role of a swan.) Just the day before, I'd sent a fake text to Sara pretending to be a guy who liked her, because I thought it would be funny. But none of those things prepared me for how it would feel to be a murderer.

"I'm sorry, Aggie," I whispered to the cracked egg I was holding in my hands. I pressed my back against the hallway wall and sank to the floor. Ever so gently, I ran one finger along the shell. It hadn't broken all the way through. "Maybe you'll still be okay." But I knew that wasn't true. Duck eggs need to gestate for twenty-eight days.

With her shell already cracked, Aggie was a goner—and it was all my fault. If I hadn't ducknapped Svenrietta, none of this would have happened. What's more, at that very moment, I would have been onstage wowing the crowd— and Connor—with my "Santa Wants a Christmas Tree" solo instead of having just called the boy I liked an idiot and embarrassing myself in front of every kid, parent, and teacher at Carleton Elementary.

A tear trickled down my cheek. Then another and another until I was bawling my eyes out and wiping away snot with the back of my hand.

That was how I was when Shady found me.

He sat down across the hall from me without a word— obviously. But Svenrietta, who was waddling along beside him, had plenty to say. She walked right over.

Wak. Wak. Wak, wak.

Don't ask how, but I could tell from her tone and the way she was looking at me that she was asking for bread and jam. Quickly, before either of them could see, I put the cracked egg behind me.

"I don't have any food for you," I said through my tears.

Shady clapped twice, and Svenri went over to settle in his lap. He started stroking her feathers gently, but the whole time, I could feel him staring at me from behind his floppy hair and through his mirrored sunglasses.

"What?!" I said finally, wiping away some of my tears. "What do you want?"

He kept right on staring.

"Okay, fine! We both know I took your stupid duck. I brought her back though."

For a minute, the only sounds in the hallway were me sniffling and Svenrietta making the little gobbling noise she makes when she preens her feathers.

"I'm sorry," I went on. "Okay. I said it. So you can stop staring at me now."

But Shady did the opposite. He reached up, raised his sunglasses, and peered out from underneath them. I'd forgotten how shiny his blue eyes were. When we were little kids, they'd always reminded me of wet pebbles on the beach.

"*What?*" I said again, pretending I didn't know, but the question he was asking with the tilt of his head was clear: *Why?*

"She was annoying me, okay?" I said. "Always quacking in class. Getting feathers all over the library. And I know you and Pouya and Svenrietta rigged the ballots for the Sock Ball *and* stole my and Rebecca's hats and put them in the lost and found. That duck's been nothing but trouble since she started school."

Shady didn't look away. It was like he didn't believe my answer.

Why?

"Okay, fine," I went on, just to get him to stop staring. "And maybe I was jealous. A bit. Once you started bringing a duck to school, you were getting so much attention...I'm kind of used to being the most popular."

That didn't do the trick either. He pushed his glasses all the way up on top of his head, wrapped his arms tightly around Svenrietta, and leaned forward. Anger flashed in his eyes.

WHY?

Honestly! What did he want from me? I didn't know why. I just did it. It wasn't planned out. But when I opened my mouth to say that, this came out instead: "Because I'm mad at you. I'm still *really* mad at you, okay?"

That seemed to surprise him as much as it surprised me. He sat back.

"We used to be really good friends. Remember the park? Making sand pancakes? And how we used to see who could run up the slide fastest? The beach house and the campfires and the Build-A-Bear birthday party where we picked matching outfits for our bears. And then you just stopped talking to me once kindergarten started. And to everyone! And after Pouya came, you only wanted to hang out with him! What did I ever do to you, anyway?"

Shady blinked slowly at me a few times.

"My mom said it was some anxiety disorder thing, and it wasn't your fault," I went on. "She said you were in therapy for it. But it still made me mad. And I missed you. It sounds stupid, but maybe that's why I stole your duck, okay?"

I didn't mean to, but I'd started crying again. Big, fat, embarrassing tears dripped down my cheeks. I had my hands over my eyes, trying to hide my ugly, blotchy face, when I felt Shady sit down beside me—the pressure of his shoulder against mine. Then I heard it:

"Shhhhhhh."

He was holding Svenrietta up, placing her gently in my arms.

"Shhhhhh," he said softly, as he settled the wriggling duck in.

The weight of her and the feeling of her breathing in and out, in and out, in and out against my chest was comforting.

The three of us sat there while I stroked Svenrietta's feathers and gradually stopped crying.

That was when Shady stood up and walked back across the hall. He stopped in front of the lost and found table. The teachers had set it up that afternoon. It was piled high with stuff for parents and kids to look through before the holidays. Shady started picking through: hats, sweatshirts, lunch bags, pencil cases. Whatever he was looking for, it was taking him forever to find it. And I was confused when, a few minutes later, he came back, sat down beside me, and handed me a piece of paper. Big parts of it were scribbled out with a black marker he must have found inside one of the pencil cases.

LOST AND FOUND TABLE

PARENTS AND STUDENTS! Please check this
lost and found table carefully for your hats, mittens,
and backpacks. All unclaimed items will be washed
and given to Goodwill in the new year.

He pointed toward Svenrietta. Then back at the paper.

Lost and found...and...for...given.

I squinted. Could it be that simple? If Shady ever dog-
napped Juliette, I'd make him my lifelong enemy. But then,
he'd always been a nicer person than me. Even back in the
sandbox.

Shady nodded.

Forgiven.

I sighed. Because he didn't know everything yet.

I reached behind my back and took out the cracked egg.
"She laid it last Monday. I was trying to keep it safe and
warm, so it would hatch, but it must have broken when
somebody moved the box onto the stage."

Shady reached out his hand, and I put Aggie into it.
Letting her go made me feel even worse, but I knew she

wasn't mine to keep. I was about to start crying again, but Shady nudged me with his elbow. I looked up. He was smiling. Not exactly the reaction to duckling murder I'd been expecting.

He got up and crossed the hall again, and because Svenrietta tried to twist out of my arms to follow him, I set her down on the floor. When Shady reached the water fountain, he turned to make sure I was watching, then he cracked the egg against the porcelain.

"Shady! Don't!" I gasped as he split it in two and emptied it into the basin.

He held the two halves of the shell up.

See?

But I didn't see at first.

See? he said again by raising his eyebrows.

I got up to look. The eggshell he was holding was empty, and in the water fountain there was nothing but some runny white stuff and a yolk. Like the eggs my parents bought at the grocery store—only a little bigger and yellower.

Aggie wasn't a duckling-to-be! She was a future omelet! Of course! The egg wasn't fertilized!

I looked down at the Lost and Found poster again, which

I'd left on the floor. How stupid had I been in *so many* ways?

"Did you really write that poem that Pouya recited?" I asked.

Shady gave a little smile. He nodded.

"It was good," I said truthfully. "I mean, even though it kind of ruined the entire play."

It seemed dumb to even think it now, but these last few years I'd been imagining Shady didn't *want* to talk anymore. That he was just being stubborn. Or, honestly, that he had nothing important to say. But he was still the same kind, funny kid I'd played with when I was four, who thought up the weirdest pretend pancake toppings (ants, acorns, and mini marshmallows made of rocks). He was still filled to the brim with thoughts and ideas. He just couldn't get them out through his mouth.

Shady sat down beside me again. Svenrietta waddled over and curled up in his lap. I reached over to pet her, and she gave a little duck sigh.

"I really am sorry," I said again.

But before Shady could give any kind of answer, Gavin and DuShawn came running down the hall in their reindeer costumes. "That play was a total disaster!" Gavin was screaming. "It's another sign. The end of the world draws ever near."

"Prepare to meet your maker!" DuShawn yelled back.

When I looked over, Shady, who still had his sunglasses perched on top of his head, was looking down the hall at the two boys, shrugging his shoulders and smiling. He picked up Svenrietta and set her in my lap again, as if to say, "It's okay. We all make mistakes." And, if I had to guess, maybe even, "It really isn't the end of the world."

CHAPTER 18

The End of the World

Told by Pouya

Maman and Mitra-Joon were pretty mad about my un-planned tree performance. Christmas isn't really a thing for most Iranian families. I always get a few presents though, so I'll feel included, and my moms threatened to return every last one of them. But in the end, they caved.

I got some clothes, books, a build-your-own replica of the Star Destroyer, and a few things that looked like they probably came from a secondhand shop. Not quite the new bike, or the PlayStation and copy of *The Evil Undead* I'd dreamed of, but no big deal. I could play video games at Shady's house. Plus, who needs more stuff when the end of the world is mere days away?

In fact, on the afternoon of December 31, as we counted down the hours to impact, Mr. Cook was on his way to pick me up. It wasn't all that cold out, and I could have walked, but the Banana Bandit was still at large. Plus, I had a lot of stuff. I was heading to Shady's for a sleepover. First, though, I bid my parents a fond (and final) farewell, which Maman mostly ignored because she was on a Skype call with Uncle Reza, and Mitra-Joon answered with "Okay, Pouya. See you tomorrow."

I had my arms loaded with end-of-the world supplies, so Mr. Cook let me in when we arrived. I was carrying my backpack, a big bag of cheese puffs, my pillow, and all the gummy worms my life savings of $41.42 could buy. I nearly dropped it all when I saw Shady.

"Huh," I said. "That's different."

He'd cut his hair. Obviously, I'd seen haircuts before, but never anything like this.

"Good different," I added. It was just a regular haircut— longer on the top and shorter on the sides, and not only was Shady's hair not falling over his eyes anymore, but his head must have been lighter, because he was standing different: straighter and more solid.

Wak, wak, wak.

Svenrietta came waddling out of the living room. She was wearing a new diaper with little Santas on it.

I don't know what Pearl Summers had fed her during the ducknapping, but when she spotted my bag of cheese puffs, she went berserk with butt wiggling. She started flapping her wings too—kind of hop-flying off the ground.

"Nuh-uh. No way," I said. "These aren't good for you." But Shady's sister, Manda, came out of the living room behind the duck.

"Oh, give her a few," she said.

"Yeah. Look how nicely she's asking," her friend Pascale pointed out from behind her new video camera—a Christmas gift from her parents.

Ever since they'd started making the duckumentary again, Pascale had been over at Manda and Shady's house a lot. I don't really get teenagers, or girls, but Manda seemed happier again. Or maybe it was just the bright scarves she'd started wearing that jazzed up her all-black outfits and made her look less witchy.

I opened the bag of cheese puffs—not because Svenrietta was asking nicely but because I realized it didn't matter.

"Sure. Why not?" Processed grains give Svenri the runs, but what was a little duck diarrhea at a time like this? We all deserved to enjoy our last moments.

Speaking of which, Shady and I had our whole evening planned. It was going to include all the best things: *The Evil Undead* from five to seven. Pizza with extra pineapple: seven to seven fifteen. More *Evil Undead* while finishing whatever was left of the gummy worms and cheese puffs: seven fifteen to eleven thirty. And all the while, we'd be keeping in close contact with the other members of the Apocalypse Preparedness Squad in case any of them had news to report.

And then, of course, just before midnight, the special ceremony. Because the end of the world only happens once, and it's worth doing right.

"You're going to get the end-of-the-world ceremony on film, right?" I asked Manda and Pascale. "I mean, what could be more dramatic than capturing the experiences of a service duck as the earth explodes?" I paused, realizing the problem with that. "Not that anyone's ever going to see it."

Pascale tried to ruffle my hair, but I ducked away in time. "Yes, we'll film your cute little ceremony," she said.

Cute? Little? I pretended I was about to strangle her, but she just laughed, and really, I didn't mind that much. I like Pascale. She's an expert at making cheese strings into octopuses, and she keeps Manda busy, so Shady and I can do whatever we want more often.

"Come on," Manda said to Pascale. "Let's take a break from filming and get some snacks."

Once the girls were gone, Shady picked up Svenri and motioned upstairs with his head. I followed, dragging along my pillow, cheese puffs, and other supplies. When we got to his room, I logged on to the group chat we'd set up with the other members of the APS: Gavin, DuShawn, Wendel, Aisha, Tammy, and Jang Hu.

How's everyone doing?

Aisha, Tammy, and Jang were together at a sleepover at Jang's apartment, which was directly upstairs from her parents' convenience store. If Planet Q happened to hit the other side of the earth—in China or something—and we were all still alive, we were going to meet there to put our survival plan into action. They sent back a picture of the three of them, holding hands and looking terrified.

Then Gavin, Wendel, and DuShawn checked in separately:

Prepared as possible with flashlights and bottled water, Gavin wrote.

A-OK so far, Wendel responded.

Dressed in fabulous end-of-the world outfit, DuShawn wrote, then he sent a picture of himself wearing a sparkly New Year's hat and a really nice dress.

After that, there was nothing to do but wait—and feed Svenri cheese puffs and eat gummy worms.

"Killer move, Captain!" I said as Shady decapitated a big boss zombie whose eyeballs were falling out of her head. But, to tell the truth, the graphic of blood and guts made me a little queasy. Up until then, I'd been pretty okay with the idea of the end of the world, but I was starting to get nervous. My stomach was flip-flopping all over the place.

Before she died, my mamani always used to go pray at a mosque in Tehran. She believed in the Day of Judgment. According to the Koran, which is a really important religious book, on the day the earth ends, Allah—or God—will judge people for the good and bad stuff they've done in their lives and send them to heaven or hell.

I wasn't sure that I believed in that, but would it be even worse if she was wrong? That would mean lights out for us all. Or what if she was right, and even helping out the other underducks at school hadn't been enough to put me on the right side of good?

As we ate pizza and played hours and hours of video games, I kept glancing nervously at the clock on Shady's bedside table. Finally it was 11:30.

"It's time," I said.

While I messaged the other members of the APS to remind them to start their ceremonies, Shady and Svenri went to get Manda and Pascale. They arrived a minute later with the video camera and some candles and matches. The ceremony got underway.

"This is so stupid," Manda muttered, but she dimmed the lights for effect, then helped Pascale adjust the settings on her new camera.

"Come on," Pascale urged. "It could be funny, at least. And if it helps us win the film competition and the trip to New Orleans, it'll be worth it."

Manda looked nervously across the room at her brother at the mere mention of the trip, but Shady nodded like, *It's okay*, and then Manda smiled at Pascale.

"Wait!" I said. "Before you start filming, I have to scatter the flours. It says so in the instructions on the Planet Q website."

"Are you sure that's what they meant by flour?" Manda frowned as she watched me take a Ziploc bag of baking flour out of my backpack.

"It's all I had!"

It was almost January! Where was I supposed to get fresh flowers? Anyway, I was pretty sure the symbolism counted more than anything.

"Okay," I said when I'd finished making a ring of flour on the carpet. "Now we all sit and hold hands inside the circle."

Manda lit the candles and placed them in the middle, then the three of us—me, Shady, and Manda—sat down and held hands. Meanwhile, Pascale filmed, and Svenri walked around the outside of the circle, trying to eat the flour off the carpet.

"Let us pray!" I said in my most serious voice. "Oh, mighty Planet Q. As you barrel toward us at unimaginable speeds, ready to smash the earth to smithereens, please have mercy on our souls."

Manda rolled her eyes.

I ignored her.

"Help to guide us out of eternal darkness and—"

AAAAAAaaaaaaahhhhh!

An earsplitting scream pierced the air, and all four of us—five, if you include Svenri—jumped.

"What was that?" Manda was squeezing the heck out of my hand.

"I think it came from outside." Pascale was already walking to the window.

"Is the world actually ending?" Manda asked with a laugh, but her voice had a thin, high edge to it.

Shady scooped Svenri up off the carpet, and we all went to look out over the street. I glanced at the clock on the way. Only 11:45! Too soon for Planet Q to make impact, and yet…

"*HELP!*" It was a lady. She sounded terrified. My stomach did a huge flop. My feet felt glued to the floor.

Shady ran down the stairs first, but by the time he reached the front door, his parents were already out in the street talking to the woman, who was wearing a purple coat.

"I was walking to my car, and he came out of nowhere, throwing bananas at me. He stole my purse," she was saying. "My wallet and car keys are inside!"

Shady's mom already had her cell phone out, calling the police.

"It was definitely the Banana Bandit," the woman said. "He was wearing that gorilla suit. It made him almost impossible to see in the dark."

While Shady's mom explained what had happened to the 911 operator, Shady's dad helped the lady inside to wait for the police. She was trembling, but when Shady brought Svenri to her and placed the duck in her arms, it seemed to distract her. We made her hot chocolate, then, together, we waited until we could hear the faint sound of sirens in the distance.

A few minutes later, two police officers stepped into the living room and shook hands with the lady. "I'm Officer Bent, and this is Officer Timone," one of them said. "Some of our colleagues are searching the area, but we'd like to ask you some questions, if we could."

I'd never been at a real, live police investigation before. I was dying to find out what was going to happen, but Shady nudged me and showed me his wristwatch: 11:58.

My stomach did its biggest flop yet. Only two minutes till the end of the earth, and I was definitely going to puke. I ran down the hall to the main-floor bathroom and wriggled the handle. It was locked.

"Just a second," Pascale called from inside. "I'm fixing my makeup."

Pascale wore a lot of makeup! And I was never going to make it to the upstairs bathroom. I ran to the front door and threw it open, with Shady following at my heels.

I only made it as far as the front steps before leaning over and releasing a torrent of rainbow-colored gummy-worm puke between Shady's mom's burlap-wrapped rosebushes.

"Ugh. Sorry." I sat back on my heels. Shady rubbed my back while I took a deep breath of wintry air and got ready to get back up. Then I froze.

I'd just caught sight of something moving ever-so-slightly in the garden. A rounded shape, like the rosebushes, only different somehow. I squinted. It was hairy.

Shady saw it too. Luckily, we didn't need words to make a plan—and, thanks to the APS, we were prepared for just such an event. I immediately thought back to a handout we'd made, "Seven Tips for Surviving the End of the World"—especially one tip we'd put in about what to do if you come face-to-face with a wild animal wandering the streets. Because if a gorilla (or a criminal dressed as one) isn't wild, I don't know what is.

Thankfully, Shady's a natural when it comes to the right response for this particular problem. If they see a mountain lion or rabid dog, most people scream or run away. That's called fight or flight. It sounds smart, but it can trigger a predator to attack. Instead, the best idea is to freeze, then move away as quietly as possible. And trust me, we froze.

Long seconds ticked by. Finally, Shady tilted his head one way—*bandit*—then the other—*door*.

I nodded and mimed tiptoeing with my fingers.

We both stood up, silent as ghosts.

"Come on," I said out loud, so the bandit wouldn't suspect he'd been spotted. "It's too cold to stay out here."

We backed into the front hall and shut the door softly behind us.

After that, things happened quickly. There was some shouting, and a chase down the street, but within minutes, Officers Bent and Timone had the bandit in cuffs and in the back of their car. In fact, it all went down so fast that I didn't even notice the time passing until the police were done taking notes, the last cop car had driven away, and

Shady's mom said we'd all had more than enough excitement for one night and sent us up to bed.

"Shady!" I pointed at his alarm clock.

It was 12:40!

It's hard to describe what I felt at that moment. Relief, partly, but also dread. I approached Shady's computer, feeling sick again, and clicked on the first message. It was from Wendel. I was fully expecting him to call me a liar-liar-pants-on-fire or at least to say, "I told you so," only…

Midnight and all is well here, he reported. **You guys okay?**

So relieved! Aisha, Tammy, and Jang had posted. **Going to bed.**

Guess the scientists were wrong! Wendel added. **It happens.**

All good, DuShawn had chimed in. **Pou? Shady? You guys okay?**

They weren't mad at me for being wrong! If anything, they were worried because—I guessed—we were friends now? There were even a few messages after that about getting together in the new year to hang out and eat some of the canned peaches we'd stashed away. Like a party.

I'll bring cut-up grapes for Svenrietta, DuShawn had promised.

And then, one by one, the members of the APS had logged off, leaving just me, Shady, and Svenrietta awake to talk about everything that had just happened.

"Well, it's a bit of a letdown," I admitted. "But at least since we're still alive, we'll have another chance to beat King Zombie tomorrow."

Shady made an agreeing face.

"And the canned-peach party will be good. Because, I swear, I'm never eating another gummy worm as long as I live."

Svenri quacked, and a splattery sound came from the general direction of her diaper.

Shady got out the supplies and started to change it, and I made a face when I saw what was inside. "I'm guessing she's never going to eat another cheese puff either," I said. "Not if you can help it."

"You know…" I went on, "they're never going to believe we helped catch the Banana Bandit when we tell them at school, right? I barely believe it myself!"

Shady nodded, then shrugged.

He was right.

"Yeah. It doesn't matter. As long as we know we did it. Who cares what anyone else thinks, right?"

Once Svenrietta's diaper was clean, Shady settled her into her crate in the corner, where she'd been sleeping ever since she got home from being kidnapped, then he got into bed.

I turned out the light and climbed into my sleeping bag.

"Night, Shady," I said into the darkness.

Everything was quiet for a bit. In fact, I was just drifting off to sleep when I heard it, small but unmistakable:

"Night, Pou."

Two Brave Boys Use Their Wits to Help Capture the Notorious Banana Bandit

ANDY McHENRY
The Fosterton Times

Pouya Fard and David "Shady" Cook, two ten-year-old boys, became unlikely heroes on New Year's Eve when the friends used their street smarts to help police take Summerside and Forest Hill's notorious purse snatcher, the Banana Bandit, into custody. The man who has robbed many victims in the area while dressed in a gorilla costume was found steps from the Cook family home. He has since been identified as Mark Richardson, a 45-year-old man from Rockport Beach. Richardson was apprehended just minutes after startling and robbing Caroline Connors, a 65-year-old woman who was walking to her car to drive home following a New Year's Eve get-together in the area.

SEE BRAVE BOYS | **A5**

AUTHOR'S NOTE

Selective mutism is a form of social anxiety. You've probably heard about the "fight or flight" response that people have in dangerous situations. But there's actually one more response that's possible: "freeze." When someone has selective mutism, their brain perceives situations where they need to speak as dangerous. Although the person is often extremely articulate and has no speech delays, in certain situations, they physically can't talk. These situations often include being at school, in public, or with extended family members.

It's a topic that's close to my heart. I was a shy child, so I wasn't surprised when my own kids were on the quiet side. However, when my daughter was seven, we realized there was more going on. One day she stopped talking almost entirely. It wasn't the result of a trauma...It just happened, and it was confusing and upsetting, especially for her, but also for some of our close friends and family members.

From making new friends to reading an eye chart at the optometrist, to ordering food at a restaurant or raising her hand in class, things most kids do without a second thought have been a huge challenge for my daughter.

But, like with any challenge, there are always opportunities hidden within. When you take away speech, other types of self-expression move to the forefront, and they can be surprising and beautiful. For my daughter, it began with visual art, then ventriloquism. (The puppet could talk for her—and that puppet was so sassy!) Then it was theater, where she could speak and even sing freely in the role of a character. And from there, she truly broke free.

For Shady, the main character in *Quack*, the journey back to speech begins with blackout poetry. By scribbling on bits of scrap paper and subtracting words, he works toward making his thoughts and wishes known. He also finds another unexpected solution in the form of a duck. Svenrietta becomes a support/service animal that helps him to move through the world with more confidence—and she soon creates a ripple effect on his friends and family as well.

According to the Anxiety and Depression Association of America, anxiety disorders affect one in eight children, and

I hope that this book won't just help to build awareness for kids who have selective mutism (which is relatively rare) but for all kids who have differences and struggles related to anxiety. At the end of the day, it's about taking one brave step at a time…and getting and giving a little help along the way.

ACKNOWLEDGMENTS

This was the toughest book I've ever written...not just because of its multiple narrators and Shady's blackout poetry (which is really fun but challenging to write! Give it a try!), but because the subject matter is so personal to myself and my family. First of all, I'd like to thank my daughter, Grace, for showing me what true bravery looks like. You've inspired me to face my own fears, time after time, to come out in better, brighter places. And Brent and Elliot: What would I ever do without you? *Mwah*, my loves!

Thanks to Amy Tompkins from Transatlantic Agency for finding this book its home and for always being in my corner; to Jonathan Westmark, a truly remarkable editor who asks all the right questions; and to the team at Albert Whitman for creating such a beautiful finished product.

Thanks also to the late Tracie Klaehn (author, psychotherapist, mother, and more) and her sidekick, Pecky the

Duck. Not only did they welcome me—a complete stranger—into their home to talk all things domesticated duck and share their cherry tomatoes…but their kindness was contagious and set the stage for the underducks theme in this book. Any and all duck-related mistakes and exaggerations found in these pages are purely my own. I'm also extremely grateful to Mitra Manouchehrian for her guidance related to the character of Pouya and his Iranian background, and to Dr. Rebecca Lubitz for her ongoing care and support of my family.

Finally, great big gratitude to the Canada Council for the Arts and the Ontario Arts Council for their generous financial support of this work.

Christine Saunders Photography

ANNA HUMPHREY has a love-hate relationship with anxiety. Hate, because its sticky grip has held her back many times, but love because it's what led her to start writing—a way to have a big, loud voice without having to say a word. She hasn't looked back since. Anna is the author of ten books for young readers, including the Megabat series and the Clara Humble series. She lives with her family in Kitchener, Ontario.